THE STAGECOACH BANDIT

A PRATT DEMPCY & COMPANY
WESTERN ADVENTURE – BOOK 1

INSPIRED BY TRUE EVENTS

ORRIS SLADE

Cover Illustration by Tamara Schmidt

Contents

Prologue

En route to Timber, California
July 1879

The smell of sweat and bergamot hovered in the stagecoach, thick and nauseating, as the heat continued to rise. One passenger, Miss Julliete Thayer, popped open her fan with a flick of her wrist to cool herself. Ripples of heat permeated off the road and wafted into the stagecoach. Budd dabbed away a trickle of sweat with his handkerchief before it had the chance to soak into his shirt collar. He listened as the married couple across from him prattled on and on about the railroad expansion.

"And then I looked at my business associate and said—" The sound of gunfire in the distance cut the man's words off.

Budd pressed a finger to his lips to silence the other passengers and watched the color drain from their faces. He stayed clear of the window and listened to the sounds outside. Budd feared the first shot had been a warning or, worse, to signal an attack. They were trapped between the Mojave Desert and the mountains. It was a perfect spot for an ambush.

Eerie silence fell over the passengers, and Budd sensed tension from the guards. Suddenly, the stagecoach lurched forward, and Miss Julliete toppled onto the floor. Muffled shouts filled the air.

Budd poked his head out the window just as masked riders came around the corner. The stagecoach rumbled as it soared over the uneven terrain. "Head for the trees at the base of the mountain," he shouted to the guards as they fired their guns. "We can lose them near the river."

"And if we don't?" one guard asked.

"If we don't, then at least we'll have more cover to defend the coach." Budd rolled up his sleeves and unholstered his pistol. He gestured with his hand, signaling the other passengers to get down as bullets pelted the side of the stagecoach.

A bullet that punched through the door struck a prospector in the chest. His brother let out a shout of alarm only seconds before he, too, was shot. Budd tried to catch the prospector's brother before he fell from the stagecoach, but one wheel hit a rock and it threw the man out.

The stagecoach ground to a stop. They'd lost a wheel.

He cursed under his breath when he saw the riders had caught up with them. There was no choice but to fight.

Budd climbed out of the stagecoach and covered the guards as they tried to hoist the stagecoach up. Another guard rolled the wheel over and attempted to force it back into its proper place. Budd aimed and fired at the bandits. He fell into a rhythm. Aim, fire, reload, and repeat. The system was like second nature to him. Bandits and raiders were something he was used to. It was conversations with polite ladies and young couples that he struggled with.

Miss Julliete screamed.

Budd's stomach dropped, and he looked over his shoulder to see the young woman gripping her arm as she whimpered. He fired six shots in rapid succession before he climbed inside the stagecoach. Budd tore the sleeve from her dress and wrapped it around the bullet wound. "Stay calm and keep pressure on that," he growled.

The force of the bullets hammering the side rocked the stagecoach.

The married man released his wife, reached beneath the bench seat, and pulled out a rifle. "How many bandits?" the man asked.

"I shot one of them. Five… six… maybe seven remain." Budd reloaded his pistol and said, "You take the left. I'll take the right."

The guards got the wheel on and the stagecoach moving once more. Budd and the married man took up their positions. Sweat burned Budd's eyes as he shot one bandit with deadly accuracy. One man rode to the front and silently lifted his hand. Budd bit down on the inside of his cheek as riders flanked the stagecoach. A bandit jumped onto the back of the stagecoach.

"They're going for the strongbox!" a guard warned.

Budd pulled himself out through the window and held on with a white-knuckled grip as the coach continued down the trail. He climbed onto the roof, but they gunned down the guard riding shotgun. "Keep going," Budd yelled. The sound of snapping reins followed his words.

He pulled himself up into a crouch, balancing on unsteady legs as the stagecoach wobbled. Budd cocked his pistol and shot a bandit trying to break the lock on the strongbox. Their leader called for a retreat. Budd fired after the four riders until his ammunition was depleted.

"Climb up here with me," the driver called.

Budd dropped onto the bench beside the driver and wiped his face. He picked up the shotgun, holding it close to his chest until a town appeared in the distance. The stagecoach pulled to a stop in front of the stables near the railroad station.

A man in a finely tailored suit approached the driver with a look of concern etched into his weathered face and asked, "What happened?"

"They attacked us. They killed two passengers and one of our own," answered the driver. "This man helped us escape."

Budd lowered himself from the bench and breathed a sigh of relief when his boots hit the ground. "I did what anyone else would have done in that situation," he replied. Budd opened the bullet-riddled door and helped Miss Julliete down from the stagecoach. "Several of your passengers and two guards were injured. People died, and there are still four bandits who got away. I hardly call that a success."

"He is being modest," the driver argued. "Mr. Mansfield fought off the bandits and helped the wounded. We wouldn't have made it here without his help."

Budd shifted on his heels uncomfortably as the well-dressed stranger walked up to him.

The man extended his hand and addressed Budd with a smile. "My name is Howard Thayer. I'm a manager with Pratt Dempcy & Company."

"Thayer…" Budd muttered in realization. The man who stood before him was Miss Julliete's father and the owner of the stagecoach. He released his hold on Miss Julliete and cleared his throat as he placed his hat upon his head.

"I seem to be short of a few guards," Mr. Thayer said. "I could use a man like you. Have you ever done security work?"

Chapter 1

Outskirts of Sacramento, California
September 1879

Six riders appeared on the horizon. Ripley Eagleson rode to the front, swathed in black like a messenger of death. He pulled down his mask and revealed a smile that had won just as many hearts as it had frightened enemies. The other riders looked on as he pointed down at the trail below.

"Any minute now, a stagecoach will appear on that road," he said with strength and confidence evident in every word. "Pratt Dempcy are thieves! They take money earned by the blood, sweat, and tears of ordinary folk like you and me, and they use it to line the pockets of their wealthy friends."

They met his words with jeers from the riders.

Rip's smile morphed into a scowl as he continued. "Now, it is our responsibility to take back that money! Our families suffer while they grow fat and complacent. That ends today!" Rip listened to the cheering as he lifted his mask once more. He addressed his men as if they were his equals, companions instead of guns for hire. And in return, they looked at him with adoration and unwavering loyalty. He was their savior.

As the voices of the riders died down, the sound of wheels turning echoed through the valley. Rip whistled beneath his mask and led his riders down the steep embankment. He watched as the stagecoach traveled along the path beside the river that cut through the valley. The guards chatted among themselves, unaware danger stalked them from afar.

Rip signaled for Johnny and Leroy to veer off to the left while he took the right. They pulled up close to the stagecoach, and screams broke through the stampede of hooves pounding against the trail.

Rip flipped his gun out of the holster and aimed at the driver. "Stop the coach!" he ordered, as Johnny leapt onto the stagecoach and yanked the gun out of the second guard's hands.

The driver looked as if he was considering an attempt to outrun them. Rip fired his gun into the air, startling the horses and stealing that courage he saw in the driver's eyes. The man trembled with fear as he pulled back on the reins. Riders surrounded the stagecoach. Rip slid his gun back into his holster and lowered himself from the saddle. Johnny held the guards at gunpoint as the others forced the passengers out of the stagecoach.

"Leroy, you take the strongbox this time," said Rip. "The rest of you search the bags for valuables." He strolled over to the people lined up on their knees near the river.

None of them had the courage to meet his gaze as he stared down at them.

"I have no interest in hurting you," Rip chuckled. "I am not a cruel man, nor am I a witless bandit. My men and I are out to right some wrongs. You folks just happened to be in the wrong place at the wrong time. Victims of circumstance, if you will."

His men tore the stagecoach apart in search of good loot. Rip heard the moment they bust the strongbox open, just before Johnny appeared at his side. John Pepper was Rip's brother-in-law. He was family, and Rip tried his best to protect him, but Johnny was often the first man in his gang to draw blood. Johnny was reckless, short-tempered, and quick with his gun. Rip knew just how dangerous his brother-in-law was, but he always gave Johnny a chance to prove himself.

"I was just telling these fine folks that we mean them no harm." Rip glared pointedly at Johnny in hopes he could get the message across. "I leave them in your care while I check on progress."

He left Johnny to guard the passengers and the three guards as he met with Leroy at the back of the stage. Leroy stuffed a few bundles of cash into his pouch, along with several nuggets of gold. Rip pulled his knife from the sheath on his belt and used it to pry open the false bottom of the oak box. Pratt Dempcy & Co started using false bottoms after Rip's crew had attacked the thirtieth of their stagecoaches. The false bottoms had worked in the beginning, but Rip had quickly figured out the company's petty tactics.

They neatly tucked away five bars of silver at the bottom of the strongbox. Rip shouted victoriously, and his men got to work, loading their bounty onto the horses. But the celebration came to a swift halt when a single gunshot rang into the valley.

Rip cursed and rushed to where Johnny stood over the driver with mischief in his emerald gaze. He smacked his brother-in-law upside the head. "Take him away!" Rip barked at Hector. "I'll deal with him later."

The gang finished packing up the loot and fled from the area as they dragged Johnny onto his horse. It was a rule among them that guns were only used if the stagecoach guards resisted. Gunshots were bound to draw attention—whether it was from the law or rival gangs—and Rip disliked any form of confrontation that ended without him getting paid. Johnny's little slipup had most likely alerted every man in the valley of their presence.

Rip shoved his boot into the stirrup and swung his leg over the saddle. He clucked his tongue, and Storm, his mount, took off toward the hill where his gang waited.

***

Iron Stallion Saloon
Sacramento

Johnny hit the ground with so much force that floorboards broke. He sat up with a groan and pressed his fingers along his tender rib cage. "I guess it's safe to assume you're a little upset," he muttered sarcastically. Johnny looked up at Rip with a droll expression on his face. "That driver had it coming, Rip."

His words fell upon uncaring ears. Most of the men in the room hated Johnny. They looked on but did nothing to intervene as the two men tussled. Rip grabbed him by the collar, yanked him to his feet, and slammed his back against the wall. Pictures fell down, exposing several feet of yellowed wallpaper and pieces of shattered glass scattered across the floor.

"I have had it with your ignorance," Rip snarled. "That kind of foolishness will get us caught someday, and then what? Huh? What happens to Kaitlyn and Beatrice when you and I are gone?"

Johnny narrowed his eyes as a roiling storm of rage brewed inside of him. He disliked the way Rip used his wife and daughter against him. Johnny was a lot of things, but he loved Beatrice with all his heart, and Kaitlyn was his little angel. They were the reason he had agreed to join Rip's gang in the beginning.

Leroy pulled Rip away from Johnny. "Stop it! If you keep making a racket, the owner will toss us out of here, and we can't afford to be seen in town yet," said the skilled lock breaker. Leroy had always been faithful to Rip—in fact, all the men seemed to worship Johnny's brother-in-law.

Rip pulled his arm back and punched Johnny square in the jaw. Johnny's teeth clicked as his head snapped to the side. He spat onto the floor and wiped away the blood from his lip. Rip had everyone fooled except Johnny. Though they saw him as the stupid brother, it was Johnny who knew all of Rip's secrets. He knew the criminal behind the charming grin and the speeches.

"You done?" Johnny asked bitterly.

Rip shrugged off Leroy's hold and adjusted his vest. "I'm nowhere near done. I want an explanation."

"The driver attempted to grab my gun," Johnny lied smoothly. "What was I supposed to do? Let him take it?"

"You could have knocked him out," Rip shouted. "You could have threatened him or beat him. Killing him when we were so close to the main road was just stupid!"

Johnny rolled his eyes and walked over to the table where a decanter of brandy sat upon a tray. He poured himself a drink, wincing when the liquor scorched a trail down his throat. "You always say that Pratt Dempcy & Company ruined your life. So what if a few guards or a driver get killed here and there?" Johnny asked.

"There is a lesson to be learned every time we attack a stagecoach." Rip took the glass from Johnny's hand and dropped it on the table with a splash. Johnny knew Rip disliked liquor or any other vice that made a man lose his wits. Rip continued, "We might be outlaws, but we are not ruthless killers."

"Honor among thieves and all that?" Johnny snorted.

Rip looked him in the eyes and sighed irritably. "Money, jewels, and expensive little trinkets are things that can be replaced. Once a human life is gone… there is no undoing it."

Johnny pulled out a chair from the table and sat down with a huff. "You and every man in this room has killed before, so don't you go starting up one of those long-winded speeches," he snapped. "We are not saints, we're sinners. Killing is killing in the eyes of God and the law. It doesn't matter when it happens or why."

Johnny never saw things in shades of gray like his brother-in-law. He had always believed the world was more black and white than Rip claimed. There had come a time in his life when lying to himself no longer helped him sleep at night. He was a husband and a father, but he was also an outlaw.

Rip leaned forward, moving his lips close to Johnny's ear, and hissed, "Step out of line again, and I'll have you tied to the whipping post." The gang leader stormed out of the room without another word.

Johnny flinched when the door slammed shut. He felt that familiar swell of reckless anger inside—the sort of anger that made him do stupid things. He waited until the tension in the room grew unbearable, then took his leave. "I'm going to get a drink," Johnny said sourly before the door closed behind him. He walked along the corridor, down the enormous staircase lined with soiled doves, and over to the bar.

Girls whistled as he walked past, and gentlemen eyed him with suspicion, but Johnny paid them no mind. He elbowed his way through the other men hanging over the bar.

The owner scowled and slid a beer over to Johnny. "Someone is here to see you. They're waitin' out back," muttered the pock-marked old man.

Johnny grabbed his beer and headed toward the back door of the saloon. The second his feet hit the dirt, someone threw him to the ground. Punches and kicks rained down upon the outlaw. He raised his arms to defend himself, but he lost count of how many times they hit him. Johnny didn't recognize his attackers as they beat him viciously. Black spots danced in his vision.

The last thing he heard before the world went dark was an angry voice that growled, "Rip hopes you got his message."

Johnny cursed through swollen lips as one last kick struck his face. He floated in and out of consciousness, unable to see or hear anything as the men walked out of the alleyway.

Chapter 2

Sacramento Valley

The last thing Budd expected when he sipped his morning coffee was the sound of gunfire. A bullet struck his cup, and the dark, bitter liquid splashed onto his lap. He jumped up with a yelp of surprise, tossing aside his coffee in favor of his gun. Budd dragged Ernest out of his seat as they nearly pelted the driver with bullets. "Highwaymen," he shouted to the other guards.

They jumped down from their perches and took cover behind the stagecoach. Luckily, there had been no passengers inside when the highwaymen appeared. Budd spotted several goons huddled behind a cluster of large rocks. They fired a constant stream of bullets at the stagecoach, leaving no room for Budd and the others to escape.

"They'll have to stop to reload," Budd said to Ernest. "When it goes quiet again, I want you to—"

A scream came from the left, and Budd saw Jonah stagger on his feet. Budd scanned his surroundings for any sign of cover for the recruit. He pointed to a large outcrop of stone nearby, and Jonah followed his command, hobbling over to take cover.

Budd shoved his gun into Ernest's hand. "I need you to lay down some cover fire while I help Jonah."

"I-is he hurt bad?" Ernest asked nervously.

"I won't know until I get over there. Just follow my lead, and everything will be okay." Budd removed his hat and grabbed his Cattleman revolver from his sidearm holster. He waited until the highwaymen ceased fire before he dashed over to the outcrop. Budd heard Ernest's attempt to cover his movements as he slid to a stop beside Jonah. "How are you holding up, kid?" he asked Jonah.

"It's bad, Mr. Mansfield!" The panicked young man looked as if he was seconds away from losing his lunch all over Budd's boots. "Tell my mama that I love her…"

Budd glanced over at the wound on Jonah's side. He snorted and pulled the bandana from his back pocket, pressing the scrap of cloth to the wound. "It just grazed you," he chuckled. "I don't think I'll be sending letters to your mother anytime soon. Just hold pressure there while I figure out how we're going to get out of this one."

Jonah seemed to calm down a bit as he peeked out from behind the outcrop. "How many are there?"

"Nine," Budd answered. "This lot has been terrorizing the roads around here for months. Usually they wait several weeks between attacks, so I thought it might be safer."

Jonah winced as he adjusted the bandana over his wound. "Just our luck, huh? We take a different road to avoid bandits, only to run into highwaymen."

Budd didn't have Jonah's sense of humor. He saw their situation as no laughing matter. "This is my fault," Budd said. "I should have scouted this area better."

"You can't control everything, Mr. Mansfield."

"Maybe not," he retorted. "But I can control how this ends."

Budd heard the fighting pick up once more. He counted the number of gunshots and stumbled out from behind the outcrop, falling over into the dirt. Silence crept over the valley. Budd held perfectly still, and his men had enough sense to do the same. He held his breath as a highwayman approached. When a hand reached down and touched his shoulder, Budd's eyes popped open.

Budd shot the highwayman in the gut before he could alert the others. He used the man's body as a shield as he fired his revolver at the rest. Ernest, Lou, and Jonah joined the fight. Chaos erupted in Sacramento Valley, and it forced the highwaymen to scatter like cockroaches when the dust settled. Budd tossed aside the body and counted the others that littered the ground.

"Let's clean up and head back to town," he said as he squatted down to help Jonah to his feet. "How much did they take?"

"Nearly everything from the strongbox," Lou replied. "I'm sorry, Budd."

"Don't be sorry. You men gave it your all. The plan didn't work, and that's on me." Budd found it hard not to take the losses to heart, for they had hired him to find new ways to defend the stagecoaches. Between bandits, highwaymen, and petty thieves, Pratt Dempcy & Co had lost a small fortune in the previous years. Since he agreed to join the company, Budd had just as many successes as he had failures.

He helped Jonah into the stagecoach and walked around back to check the extent of the damage. Repairing the stagecoach would no doubt cost a pretty penny, but the real problem was the company had to pay an insurance fee to their clients each time a robbery occurred. Budd finished up his assessment and climbed onto the stagecoach. He didn't say a word to the others as they drove into town.

Sheriff Dawson was at the stables when they arrived in Sacramento. Budd greeted the sheriff as usual, but the worried expression on the man's face struck him as odd. Sheriff Dawson had earned a reputation as a man with a cool disposition, usually unfazed by the crimes that had happened in town.

"Something on your mind, Sheriff?" Budd heard himself ask. He saw no harm in lending Dawson a hand, though he still had supplies to pick up from the shops before heading back on the road.

"A man came into the office this morning and filed a report. He said a stagecoach was attacked just south of town about three days ago." Dawson scratched at his chin as that worried expression worsened. "A group of bandits robbed the passengers and emptied the strongbox. They killed one of the drivers in cold blood. Strangely, the man didn't seem too upset about it…"

"How so?"

"Though he was rattled by the driver getting shot, he said the leader of the bandits treated them fairly," Dawson muttered. "I've never known a bandit to be polite, let alone fair."

Budd could see why the sheriff seemed so confused. "Let me get Jonah to the doctor, and then I'll ride out there with you," he replied. "Maybe one of us can make some sense of this."

***

Outskirts of Sacramento

Budd looked down at the ground, where the trail was still stained with the driver's blood. He picked up the casing of a bullet near the parallel lines left behind by the wheels of the stagecoach. Budd expected to find drag marks where the coach might have skidded off the trail, muddled tracks, or even tufts of torn clothes. There were at least four sets of footprints, but there was nothing that indicated a fight may have occurred, much less a robbery. "There wasn't a struggle?"

"The bandits were in and out quickly," replied Sheriff Dawson. "A man threatened the driver, and the guards thought it best to comply with the order to stop the stagecoach."

Budd nodded and glanced around at the surrounding hills. He wondered how the ambush might have played out. "Any witnesses that could identify the bandits?" he inquired with a furrowed brow. "A gang that can rob a stagecoach in under ten minutes without so much as a single stone out of place is hard to believe."

Sheriff Dawson unfolded a piece of paper before he handed it over to Budd. "Read it yourself," the sheriff suggested. "There is no way to identify the men. All we have to go on is the guard's word and a tattoo of an eagle."

Someone had written down a sloppy description, retelling the events that had taken place during the robbery. Budd thought back to the attack that led to his employment with Pratt Dempcy & Company. "Masked riders swathed in black," Budd read out loud. "Blood-red masks covered their faces."

"Does that sound familiar to you?" Dawson questioned.

The bandits that attacked the stagecoaches in the past had worn black clothing and concealed their identities behind cotton masks colored in a deep shade of red. Was it the same group of bandits attacking the stagecoaches? Budd wondered to himself. He shook his head and shrugged, even as a knot had formed in the pit of his stomach. It was impossible for Budd to be sure without more information.

"Perhaps. What sort of strongbox did the stagecoach carry?" he asked Sheriff Dawson.

"Standard oak with iron hinges and a reinforced lock." The lawman crossed his arms over his chest and met Budd's stare evenly. "The bandits could break in and take the contents without damaging the strongbox itself. No scuff marks, dents, or scratches."

"They either have a key to the lock, or they got their hands on some kind of locksmith tool," Budd grumbled. He pinched the bridge of his nose and handed back the witness report to Dawson. "I want to look into this more. Maybe track down a lead on the tattoo. If it's all right with you, of course..."

"Be my guest." Sheriff Dawson's shoulders slumped, and for a moment, Budd could see just how exhausted the man was. "To be honest with you, I have my hands full as it is.

Being the new sheriff in town makes people want to test your patience."

Budd patted Dawson's arm. "You'll get the hang of it," he said. "I can see you do good work. You've earned my respect, Sheriff, and you'll eventually earn the respect of your town."

They surveyed the area a bit longer before riding back to Sacramento. Budd wasted no time when he arrived at the stables and hurried inside to look at the stagecoach that was attacked. He nodded his head to the men tending the horses, but he kept his eyes sharp and his mind on the job. Budd ran his hands along the doors, feeling for bullets that might have gotten lodged in the wood. The search seemed fruitless until Budd's hand grazed something odd while feeling along the contours of the driver's bench.

He pulled the object free and saw it was an ace of spades that had been pinned to the bench with a throwing knife. The card triggered something inside of Budd. It was strangely familiar to him. He wondered to himself why the bandits had been so careful, only to leave behind the card.

Many of the gamblers Budd met in the past had informed him of a superstition about the ace of spades. Some believed when it wasn't accompanied by the rest of the deck, the ace of spades was a symbol of death. Others had said the card was lucky to the man who played it, bringing him riches and prosperity. Budd figured both explanations were accurate enough. He understood why a gang might have been inspired to use the card as their signature.

"Looking for something?" Lou asked from over Budd's shoulder.

Budd straightened to his full height and held up the card for Lou to see. "Did you see something like this the day they attacked us back in July?"

'On our way to Timber?' Lou cocked his head as he took a moment to think. The curious driver always reminded Budd of a dog with its ears perked up. Lou snapped his fingers suddenly and said, "Yep. There was an ace of spades in the back. Stuck there by a knife of some sort. I turned it over to Mr. Thayer when I handed in my report."

Budd ran out of the stables before Lou had even finished his sentence. He hurried along the sidewalk, weaving between the folks who moseyed about town. Budd burst inside the post office, entered the telegram room near the back, and slammed his hand down on the telegraph operator's desk.

Newman should have been used to Budd's commanding presence by now, but the operator still jumped in his seat at the loud bang. "At least give me time to adjust my spectacles before you get to barkin' at me," he snapped. He and Budd often bickered, but their friendship was genuine.

"I need you to get a message to Mr. Thayer. It's urgent," Budd replied, ignoring Newman's blathering.

"Everythin' with you is urgent," griped the operator.

Budd grabbed a pen and jotted down his message. He was careful not to leave out any details and paid Newman a little extra to prioritize his telegram.

Chapter 3

Haven Ranch

Rip opened the front door to Beatrice's home and was greeted by the smell of roast beef and gravy. His sister always cooked a delicious meal for the family on Sundays after church. There was nothing like home-cooked food and time with his niece Kaitlyn to take his mind off of Johnny's foolishness. Rip peeled off his coat and gently laid it across the back of a nearby chair.

He smoothed a hand over his vest before he wandered into the kitchen. Beatrice hummed a happy little tune as she stirred a simmering pot on the stove. Kaitlyn snickered mischievously. Rip glanced over and bit back a chuckle as the young girl poked holes in the biscuits when her mother wasn't looking. He crept up behind Kaitlyn and tugged on her long braid, causing her to let out a squeal when he startled her.

Kaitlyn whirled around with a smile. "Uncle Rip!" the young girl cheered.

Rip kissed his niece on the cheek. "How was Pastor Murphy's sermon?" he asked. To his absolute joy, Kaitlyn was at an age where she had the tendency to ramble on for hours. Rip was happy to just sit and listen to her stories as Beatrice set the table. His sister sighed with exhaustion, but there was a fond smile on her face when she looked at her daughter.

Johnny entered the kitchen through the back door. Rip smiled to himself as he looked upon the black and blue splotches that obscured his brother-in-law's features. The yellowed edges around the bruises showed that Johnny had started healing nicely over the past three days. Rip hoped the message had gotten through Johnny's thick skull once and for all.

"Rip," Johnny said nervously.

"John," replied Rip, as he carried Kaitlyn into the dining room and set her down in the chair beside his seat. He thanked his sister for the lovely meal.

Beatrice took her place beside her husband, wise enough to stay out of the conflict that brewed between the two outlaws. Rip glared at Johnny down the length of the table and grasped Kaitlyn's hand to say grace. Her soft voice repeated the words she had learned in church, filling the uncomfortable silence with prayer.

"Let's eat!" Johnny whooped when Kaitlyn finished up.

Rip lifted his fork to his mouth and hummed in appreciation when the savory roast hit his tongue. "Perfect as always, Beatrice. Mama would be proud that you mastered her old recipe."

"Feeding my family is only possible because of you, Ripley," Beatrice said as she beamed over at her brother. "We were in a dark place before you came back to Sacramento."

"When my darling little sister sends me a letter about struggling to get food on the table..." Rip slapped his hand on top of the table before continuing, "Then, by God, it is my job to set things right."

He basked in the adoration of Beatrice and Kaitlyn, but Johnny's posture was filled with tension. Rip thought it reminded him of a viper getting ready to strike. He refused to let Johnny's sour mood destroy their lovely night. Rip ignored Johnny and started telling a story about one of his grand adventures. He left out all the blood and banditry for Kaitlyn's sake.

"There I was, with nothing but my side arm and a single bullet, staring into the eyes of one of them darn Pinkertons!" Rip said excitedly.

Beatrice cleared the table with a glimmer of fascination in her eyes as she listened to the story.

Rip lowered his voice to a whisper and continued, "They had me backed into a corner with nowhere to go... and then... BAM!"

Kaitlyn jumped in her seat before bursting into a fit of giggles. "What happened?"

"A wagon crashed into a tree nearby," he explained. "It distracted the Pinkertons for only a second, but I knew it was my chance to get out of there."

"You ran?" Kaitlyn gasped.

"I ran as far and as fast as my feet would allow. Nothing could have kept me from you and your mother when you needed me most." Rip finished up his story and then said goodnight to his niece.

Beatrice and Kaitlyn walked up the stairs and disappeared into the corridor. The moment they faded out of sight, Rip grabbed Johnny by the back of his shirt. He dragged his brother-in-law out the back door and threw him to the ground.

Johnny leapt to his feet with a sneer. "Are you out of your mind?"

Rip pushed his hair out of his face and shook his head. "No," he replied. "I'm not out of my mind. In fact, I'm glad you showed up tonight, John. It's important for you to see that Beatrice and Kaitlyn need someone to protect them."

"Is this about that driver I killed?" Johnny griped. "When are you going to let that go?"

"I have a bounty on my head big enough to make a preacher feel tempted," Rip snapped back. "Every time I have to clean up your mess, it brings us all closer to the hangman's noose. Look around you. Look at what is at stake if you mess up again."

"So what? You plan to beat me every day until I fall in line?" Johnny asked as he went to punch Rip, but the gang leader was too quick.

He went to grab Johnny again, but the bandit sidestepped his advance and punched Rip in the side. The sheer audacity of Johnny's brazen actions hit harder than the blow itself. Rip head-butted Johnny so hard his teeth rattled from the impact. Johnny was knocked out almost instantly, dropping like a sack of rocks.

"Hit me again and I'll kill you," Rip threatened.

***

Budd stabbed out his cigarette and finished his coffee as the sun appeared over the mountains. He watched a train roll into the station at the edge of town. Mr. Thayer was one passenger on board. The ride from Timber to Sacramento was short but unpleasant.

With the roads unsafe, folks had to spend a pretty penny for a train ticket, and the sweltering heat outside made the passenger cars stifling. Budd didn't envy the folks on board. He grabbed his hat and headed out of his room. A woman in the corridor giggled as he walked by, blushing like a schoolmarm with a crush. Budd slid her a smile and carried on toward the front desk of the hotel.

The owner greeted Budd with a wide grin. "Mornin', Mr. Mansfield," said the owner. "How was your stay?"

"My stay was fine, as always. I'll be back tonight. Save a room for me." Budd stepped outside and into the light of day. A horse trotted by with its rider slouched over the saddle after what Budd assumed was a long night at the saloon. He shook his head with a disgruntled sigh as he strolled along the sidewalk. Mr. Thayer's striped city suit was unmistakable, even in the crowd of people who arrived on the train.

It took a moment for Mr. Thayer to recognize Budd without his beard and overgrown hair. "Budd, dear boy!" called Mr. Thayer. "So good to see you, lad. I was just singing your praises to a young widow on the train."

"I'm sure she was lovely, but I'm not looking for that sort of thing right now," Budd said as he felt the heat of his blush. "I would much rather discuss business, if you wouldn't mind."

"Ah, yes! I read your telegrams, and my associates and I have come to a conclusion." Mr. Thayer shuffled over to a bench outside the general shop. He set down his briefcase and opened it with a snap. Budd looked over his employer's shoulder and saw what appeared to be an amendment to his contract.

"What's all that?" he asked. "Am I in some sort of trouble?"

"Golly, no. In fact, we would like to offer you a position as the manager of security." Mr. Thayer sifted through the papers and found the contract. "You were a lawman in the past, if I'm not mistaken…"

"Something like that," Budd grumbled. He disliked dwelling on the past. After all, he had journeyed to Sacramento for a fresh start, like so many others.

"Splendid! We want you to focus your attention on finding the man with the tattoo," replied Mr. Thayer. "Hunt down leads, fight off bandits—I do not care what you have to do! Just do whatever it takes to make this problem go away. You have the full support of Pratt Dempcy & Company behind you."

Bud wasn't easily convinced. "What about the job up north? I was supposed to get supplies and then help guard the transport—"

"Never mind about that," Mr. Thayer insisted. "Find the bandits who keep attacking our stagecoaches. The fate of the company rests on your shoulders."

He was not sure how to respond to Mr. Thayer's words. Budd stared down at the contract in his hand and at the added clause that stated his additional responsibilities. Times were hard, but Budd never thought the day might come where he was asked to save the company. "How bad has it gotten?" Budd asked.

A shadow crossed Mr. Thayer's face. His shoulders slumped and patted Budd on the arm. "Bad enough that we have made this a top priority," answered Mr. Thayer. "It makes no difference how many clients choose to travel in our coaches if they are robbed before they arrive at their destination!"

A few people slowed as they passed by, turning to look at Budd and his employer. Mr. Thayer cleared his throat and pulled Budd over to the eatery beside the post office. They ordered some breakfast before Budd replied.

"I haven't been with the company long. Sometimes I feel like there's more to this than you are telling me, and I can't do my job until I know the whole truth."

Mr. Thayer dabbed away the sweat on his brow with a handkerchief. "I am not sure what you are expecting to hear," he said. "All I can tell you for certain is that your findings at the most recent attack were what I needed to prove that it was one gang behind these robberies."

"And you believe the man with the tattoo I mentioned might be the leader?" Budd questioned skeptically.

"That or he may point us in the right direction." Mr. Thayer took a bite of his breakfast and handed Budd a pen. "You have a choice in this. You can take that job up north, or we can take these thugs down together."

Budd took the pen in his hand. His eyes flickered between Mr. Thayer's impassive expression and the contract on the table. He breathed deeply for several minutes.

It would have been so easy to push the contract away and take that ride up north, but Budd's past kept calling to him like a siren's song. He had always had a sharp instinct with finding answers.

"I heard a while ago that people back east think outlaws are mysterious and exciting—romantic, even," he began. "Personally, I think they're just a bunch of fools making mistakes. They all get sloppy. And when that happens... I like to be there to see them pay for their crimes." Budd signed his name at the bottom of the contract and handed it back to his employer.

Chapter 4

A fire had sparked in Budd's spirit. A long time had passed since he felt the thrill of the chase. He knocked on the front door of Mrs. Lisa Cornwall's home. The door opened slowly and a pale hand holding a revolver appeared. "Don't you come any closer!" said the woman just inside the entrance. "I don't want any trouble around here."

"Are you Lisa Cornwall?"

"I am." A mane of brown waves popped out the door. "Who's askin'?"

"My name is Budd Mansfield, Mrs. Cornwall," Budd answered. "I just need a moment of your time. You see, I'm working with Sheriff Dawson and the stagecoach company to find out who might be behind the attacks."

The gun lowered, and Mrs. Cornwall allowed Budd inside her home. It was nothing special, with simple furniture, bare walls, and wood floors. "My husband and I already talked to the sheriff the day it happened," she explained.

"And I understand you saw a tattoo of an eagle on one man?" Budd pulled out a small notepad and a pencil. He set them down on the table in the entrance hall. "Could you perhaps draw me a picture?"

Lisa Cornwall shrugged before she drew what she remembered of the tattoo. She sketched the image of an eagle devouring a snake onto the paper. "I saw this on the wrist of the mean one," she said. "I ain't much of an artist, so you'll have to excuse the drawin'. It won't be hung up in a museum, that's for sure."

"Mean one?"

"The rest of the outlaws were quiet," she explained. "It was hard to keep track of who was who, but there was one outlaw that seemed to anger the others. He was rather… unstable. The others were upset that he killed the driver."

"And he was the man with the tattoo?" Budd asked.

"Yes. My husband claimed it was John Pepper."

"Did it seem as if he was the leader of the gang?" He picked up the drawing when Mrs. Cornwall was finished.

"Goodness, no," she chuckled. "The man in charge was very polite. He had no intention of hurtin' any of us."

That was not the first time he had heard witnesses call the bandit leader polite, charismatic, or even generous. Just a few weeks back, Budd investigated a stagecoach robbery where the passengers had been given water as they waited in the desert.

"Is there anything else you might be able to tell me?" Budd asked. "Perhaps something unusual you noticed during the robbery."

Mrs. Cornwall tapped her chin lightly with the tip of her finger as she considered his question. "Come to think of it… the man in charge told us his gang was out to right some wrongs," she said. "Not sure I can be any more of a help."

"You've done great, Mrs. Cornwall. Thank you." Budd tucked the drawing into his pocket and walked out the front door with a tip of his hat.

Budd questioned people all over town, but none of them were as forthcoming as Mrs. Cornwall. The barber completely refused to acknowledge Budd. The doctor had slammed his door in Budd's face, and the man who worked at the post office replied with little more than a few grunts of disapproval. Finally, Budd's search brought him to the Iron Stallion Saloon.

The swinging doors opened with a squeak as Budd swaggered inside. His height and size often caused heads to turn when he was in town. A few men muttered quietly among themselves when he was forced to duck his head to pass through the doorway. The bartender sucked his teeth and wiped down the counter with a filthy rag.

Budd knocked on the bar. "I'll have a beer and a moment of your time, please," he said casually.

"What do you want?"

"Have you seen a man with this tattoo?" Budd asked as he slid Mrs. Cornwall's drawing over to the barkeep. "He might go by the name of John Pepper."

"You a bounty hunter?" growled the bartender.

"Does he have a bounty to hunt?"

"I ain't got no answers for you." The man tossed the drawing back at Budd. "Best stop askin' questions and carry on before trouble comes knockin' at your door."

Budd tilted his head and leaned over the bar. "That a threat or a warning, friend?"

Suddenly, a stranger clapped Budd on the shoulder and steered him toward a table near the back of the establishment. Budd barely had time to react before someone shoved him into a chair.

A large, burly man with dark hair and even darker eyes glared at him from beneath a tattered old hat. "You trying to get yourself killed?" asked the stranger.

"Who are you?"

"The name is Evan Farris." He sat down across from Budd and removed his hat. The man's tawny complexion made Budd wonder whether he was part of a local tribe. "I know everything about everyone, and I know how to get my hands on things that aren't exactly legal in these parts."

Budd shook his head and said, "I want nothing to do with a conman and a fence."

"Hey, now," Evan replied. "I just saved you from an early grave. The man you're looking for knows some powerful people. He's got a demon watching his back, and you would do well to tread carefully."

There was something about Evan's amiable smile that both charmed and annoyed Budd. He'd humor the sly criminal if it meant finding answers about the bandits. "You said you know everything about everyone? Well, I'm a professional problem solver, and the man with this tattoo is a problem."

Evan took the drawing from Budd's hand and traced it with his finger. A flash of recognition appeared in the depths of those dark eyes. "Listen here, partner," Evan said. "Have a drink with me down at the Parlor Room. It's a place near to here, and you'll find a friendlier crowd than this lot."

"I want answers."

"You'll get them after you buy me a drink." Evan stood up and sauntered toward the back door of the saloon with the drawing in hand.

Budd had no choice but to follow him outside. He snatched the drawing from Evan and put it safely in his satchel. "One drink and then we talk."

***

Parlor Room
Sacramento

Evan Farris was one hell of a drinker. One beer turned into two, two turned into three, and then the rest was nothing more than a blur by the time Budd looked at the clock. He wasn't much of a drinker, but Evan proved to be a very persuasive guy.

Budd hobbled over to one of the game tables with a beer clutched in each hand. Budd dropped five dollars onto the green cloth-covered table, with hiccups bursting from his lips. "I'll play a couple of rounds," he slurred. "Hope you fellas like losing. I know my way around a poker table." He looked over his shoulder for a moment and saw his drinking partner near the stairs.

Evan danced a little jig with one of the painted ladies who worked at the establishment, twirling her around until he stumbled. Budd cheered them on as he blindly bet on cards he could barely see in his inebriated state. The music seemed far too loud and yet too quiet at the same time.

They gambled, danced, and hollered like a pack of wild animals. More and more people joined in their merriment as the night went on. Budd's head spun wildly. His tongue tasted foul, as bile burned the back of his throat. He drank one more beer to wash it down and nearly tripped over Evan's dancing feet.

Budd cackled loudly before colliding with another patron. "Sorry, friend. I was—"

The man punched Budd in the mouth, silencing his explanation before he could finish. Evan saw Budd stagger back and jumped into the fight. Two more men joined the brawl as well. Budd tossed someone over the poker table. Chips and dollars went soaring into the air. The music cut off just as Evan slammed his opponent into the piano. A jangly melody echoed through the Parlor Room.

Budd took a blow to the stomach. Nausea made dark spots dance in his vision. When he recovered, Budd grabbed a bottle from behind the bar and smashed it over one of the brawler's heads. Glass sprayed across the floor. It stopped at the feet of an angry-looking gentleman.

The man stormed over and pushed Evan toward the door. "You and your friend have had enough," he shouted. "Get out of here and don't come back until you've learned how to conduct yourselves in a more civilized manner."

The owner's sons tossed the two unlikely comrades out on their hind ends. Evan leaned against Budd as he brushed himself off. "Come on, partner. Let's sober up and have that talk."

"Sounds good to me," Budd replied. "I can feel a headache coming on already."

They ended up at an inn that was cleverly named Just A Bed. Budd couldn't help but think the name was more than appropriate when he saw the barren room Evan had rented. It was nothing more than four walls, a bed, a chamber pot, and a small table that was barely the width of Budd's thigh. Evan used it as a place to mix up their coffee. It was cold and bitter, but it cut through the fog that lingered in their minds from the beer.

"Remind me to kill you in the morning," Budd groaned. He rubbed his eyes and stared around the room before he noticed Evan had become very serious suddenly.

"Do you believe in destiny, Budd?"

"A bit," Budd replied. "The day I joined Pratt Dempcy felt like a call from fate. I had told myself a fresh start was all I needed, that all I had to do was keep moving until I found where I belonged. The stagecoach company gave me more than just a job... It gave me purpose. Why? What's on your mind?"

Evan set down his coffee and slid down the wall. He didn't stop until he was sitting on the floor with his legs stretched out. "John Pepper and I grew up together. He was always getting into trouble, but we were friends, you know?"

Budd nodded, along with Evan's explanation.

"When he joined up with a local gang of outlaws, I distanced myself," Evan whispered. "We went three years without talking. Not a single spoken word or letter. But then, suddenly, that same gang of outlaws raided our hometown. My wife and son were among those who were killed."

"My goodness. That... I can't imagine how that feels. I'm sorry, Evan." Budd understood then why Evan had insisted on the drinks. It must have been extremely difficult to say such things out loud.

"It was Johnny who killed them," Evan revealed. "He was seen running out of my house with an arm full of my wife's jewelry."

Budd watched a tear slither down Evan's cheek. "Come on. Let's get you to bed." He stood up from where he sat on the edge of the mattress, walked over to Evan, and helped his new friend up. Budd laid Evan on the bed and tossed the covers over him. He wanted Evan to sleep off the rest of the liquor in his system.

Once Evan's eyes were closed for the night, Budd curled up on the floor with only his satchel for a pillow. He listened to the faint snores that reverberated off the walls. His sore jaw was proof the night had gotten a little out of hand. But Budd couldn't remember the last time he had laughed so hard. Evan was the closest thing Budd had to a friend in years, despite only knowing the enigmatic man for a few hours.

Still, Budd was eager to find out what Evan knew about John Pepper and the bandits who attacked the stagecoaches.

Chapter 5

Rip breathed in the earthy flavor of his cigar until his lungs burned. He looked down at the valley below and grinned from ear to ear when a stagecoach appeared. "You know the rules, boys," Rip said to his men. "Do not kill anyone unless you have no other choice." He snapped the reins and headed down the hill toward the trail.

Johnny and Leroy rode up beside Rip as he tugged a red mask over his mouth. The gang circled the stagecoach near the fork in the road, cutting off the horses before they could make the turn. The guard grabbed his shotgun and aimed right at Rip's head. Two more guards readied their weapons on top of the stagecoach.

Rip cursed beneath his mask. "There's only four of you," he said calmly. "And there's six of us. How far do you reckon you'll get before my men pelt you with bullets?"

Johnny pushed up his sleeves and twirled his big hunting knife. One guard caught sight of the movement. "It's them!" the man barked. "The one with the tattoo is with them." There was barely a second of hesitation before the guards opened fire.

Rip jumped off the back of his horse as the shotgun cocked. He hit the dirt with a loud thud and crawled on his belly toward an outcrop. The shotgun blast tore through the leather of the saddle, startling his mount. His men fired their guns as the stagecoach tore off down the path. Rip whistled for his horse, lifted himself back into the saddle, and gave chase. The rhythm of the pounding hooves against the ground matched his frantic heartbeat.

Storm tossed his mane. Rip murmured comforting words to his mount as they caught up with the stagecoach. Johnny and Hector were on top of the coach. The guards put up a good fight, but that distracted them from Leroy breaking open the strongbox in the back. Two more of Rip's men snatched luggage from the roof.

Rip shot the harness that tethered one horse to the stagecoach. The horse bucked and forced the coach off the path. Rip laughed evilly as the horses stumbled over one another and the stagecoach flipped on its side. Passengers screamed. Johnny and Hector spewed a few lines of colorful profanity. They recovered quicker than the guards did.

"On your mounts! Now!" Rip ordered.

He held the guards at gunpoint as his men got away with the loot. When the driver regained consciousness, Rip tossed him a coin purse. "Use that to pay for the damage. I don't want it coming out of your wages," he said. "Wait until we're gone before you grab them horses. It's nothing personal, fellas."

The guard stared down at the coin purse that landed beside him. Instead of picking it up, he spat at the ground near Storm's hooves in a blatant show of disrespect. "I don't take money from thieves."

Rip had half a mind to shoot the man dead. Instead, he left the money where it was and returned to his gang. The rendezvous point was near a large oak tree that stood tall and proud at the top of a hill. Hector tore open the bags of luggage in search of valuables while Leroy counted the stacks of cash taken from the strongbox.

Rip pulled his horse to a stop and threw a punch that knocked Johnny on his bottom. "They recognized you!" the gang leader shouted. He tossed aside his hat and tugged on the greased back strands of his hair. "Seven years you boys have been riding with me, and not once have we been recognized."

Johnny looked as if he wanted to say something. He wiped the blood from his lip and wisely kept his mouth shut as Rip flew off into a rage.

"Those marks of an eagle are a sign of solidarity! Of the brotherhood within this gang! They are a symbol of the legacy I hope to leave behind for all of you... the promise I made to protect you with my name and reputation." Rip paced beneath the tree. "Johnny here has gone and tainted that profound meaning. It is now a means by which the law can hunt us and persecute us for doing nothing more than trying to survive."

"What do we do?" Leroy asked as he looked around at the other men before his gaze landed on Rip. "The stagecoach company has a new man workin' for them. He's been askin' questions around town. If he finds out—"

"He won't," Rip said. "Because Johnny will take care of it."

"I will?" Johnny asked in confusion as he limped over to Rip. "I was thinking I would lay low and stay out of town for a while."

"No, you are going to be a man for once in your miserable life and clean up your own mess. I'll be up at the cabin, staying quiet for a few days. Send word when this situation is dealt with." Rip grabbed Johnny by the back of his neck and squeezed. "And if I hear my name has been on your lips..."

The threat remained unspoken. There was a distinct tension in the air as the men turned their gazes away from Rip and Johnny. Their loyalties rested with the leader of the gang, the man who kept their families safe. Rip removed his hand from Johnny's neck. He clapped Hector on the shoulder and squatted down beside the bag that contained their loot. It wasn't a bad take, but it wasn't enough to get them out of the region.

***

"Rise and shine!"

Budd lurched up off the floor and banged his shin against the bed frame. He swallowed down a curse as the pain in his leg only worsened his throbbing headache. Budd squinted around the room, blinking like a sleepy owl as he caught sight of Evan Farris. Memories of their night flashed in Budd's mind, and he let out a pained groan. "You said one drink," he grumbled. "I feel like I've got a pickax buried in my skull."

"What can I say, friend? I'm a man of vices. It ain't in my nature to deprive any man of a good time." Evan pranced around the room as if he was entirely unfazed by their drinking. "And while you were snoozing away the morning light, I was putting in work."

Budd snorted. "I find it hard to imagine you doing any sort of honest work."

"I said work," Evan replied. "Said nothing about it being honest. Anyway, I came up with a plan. I'll help you find the gang if you convince your sheriff buddy to forget about that small bounty on my head and let me take down John Pepper."

"Out of the question." Budd stood up once his head stopped spinning. He snatched up his abandoned cup of coffee and gulped down the thick slug left in the cup. The heat in the room had nearly evaporated all the water.

Evan shuffled over to Budd's side. He held his hands up, gesturing wildly as he spoke. "You and I make a great team! With my smarts, devilishly handsome looks, and your… guns… that gang won't stand a chance. I'm hunting down Pepper, and you're after his gang. It only makes sense that we work together on this." Evan grabbed the cup from Budd's hand with a grimace. He slammed it back on the table as his expression became less cunning and more sincere. "All I'm asking is for a chance to avenge my family."

Budd squeezed his eyes shut for a moment. He understood Evan's desire, but he had no intention of making himself accountable for someone else's life. "I'm sorry, Evan," Budd said after a short while. "More people could get hurt, and I don't want you tied up in this."

"You need me," Evan said earnestly. "No one around here is going to talk to an outsider, Budd. They can't get you close to John the way I can."

Budd shook his head once more. "The stagecoach company won't hire someone with a bounty, and the sheriff is a straight shooter. He's as by the book as they come," he replied evenly, trying to get Evan to see reason. "There's nothing I can do."

"Then let me help, anyway. No one has to know except me and you. Leave the officials out of this."

The look in Evan's eyes as he begged weakened Budd's resolve. Back when he had nothing to offer, Pratt Dempcy & Company had taken a chance on him. "All right," he said, only to cut Evan off before he got too excited. "But we do this the right way. I'll talk to my superiors and the sheriff. If they agree, we go after John and the gang together."

Evan did a little happy dance as he clapped his hands. "Woohoo! You and me! This will be quite the adventure, friend. They'll be writing stories about us, like one of them dime novels."

"Calm down. No one has agreed to anything yet," Budd griped even as a slight smile curled on his lips.

He gathered up his things and left Evan at the inn with the promise to return. The town was bustling at midday. Budd brushed past strangers on the sidewalk, wondering if any of them were part of the gang responsible for the stagecoach attacks. It wasn't paranoia exactly, but Budd couldn't shake the feeling that there was someone watching him. Someone with a wicked vendetta. He cut across the road after a wagon passed by and dipped inside the sheriff's office.

Mr. Thayer glanced up from the file in his hand and greeted Budd with a smile. "Good morning, son. How is the investigation coming along?"

"That's what I've come to talk to you about—the both of you."

Sheriff Dawson arched a thick brow and cleared his throat. Budd's attention shifted between the lawman and the stagecoach manager. There was a knowing look in Dawson's eyes. No doubt the sheriff had heard all about Budd and Evan's night of bonding.

"I've met with a... consultant," Budd said as he continued.

Mr. Thayer scratched at his chin and muttered, "Consultant?"

"Yes, well, actually, he's more of an informant than a consultant." Budd shifted nervously just inside the entrance to the sheriff's office. He removed his hat and wiped away the sweat that threatened to spill into his eyes. "A man by the name of Evan Farris. He's very knowledgeable about the gang behind the attacks. I think he can help us find the man with the eagle tattoo. Maybe even the leader of the gang."

"Evan Farris?" Sheriff Dawson's face turned a bright shade of red. The lawman stood up with such a force that his chair scraped across the floor before toppling over. "Farris is a wanted man, Mr. Mansfield. He's nothing more than a thief who hides behind slick words and a—"

"With all due respect, Sheriff, Evan Farris has been up front with me from the moment we met," Budd said. "He admitted to having a bounty on his head, and yet he's willing to risk his freedom—perhaps even his life—to help me find these dangerous men."

Mr. Thayer spoke up to support the sheriff. "I'm sorry, but I cannot allow a man of Mr. Farris's ill repute to work for our company. Pratt Dempcy has a reputation to uphold, and being associated with a known criminal could be detrimental to our future."

Sheriff Dawson pressed his lips into a tense line. He breathed deeply through his nose and then exhaled sharply. "If he causes any trouble, no matter the severity of the crime, my men will arrest him immediately," he warned. "I make no exceptions to the law, Mr. Mansfield. Farris isn't wanted in Sacramento, so I can't lay a finger on him without the government's permission. But I promise you, if I see anywhere him near the stagecoaches or any of the witnesses, I will put him behind bars."

Chapter 6

Haven Ranch

Sacramento

Budd hadn't the heart to tell Evan what the sheriff and Mr. Thayer's decision had been. There was more to the man's story than most folks could understand. Before making his way out of town, Budd did some research on his new friend. It turned out Evan Farris had jumped aboard a moving train to confront John Pepper over the death of his family. Things seemed to have gone sour, and Evan ran from the law after a brief shootout with his sworn enemy.

One poor decision had turned a good man into an outlaw.

Budd figured it hadn't all been bad, though. Evan had made a name for himself, using his unsavory reputation to his advantage as he searched for John Pepper. Evan was resourceful. Budd just hoped their newfound alliance proved beneficial for the both of them. After all, taking this chance on Evan was sure to put Budd's job on the line.

He was waiting near a small cattle ranch on the outskirts of town for Evan to arrive. The modest homestead was registered with the bank under the name of Mrs. Beatrice Pepper. Budd had slipped the bank manager ten dollars to look at the contract. Sure enough, it was on record that John Pepper was Beatrice's husband and a cosigner for the ranch. Whether it was the tattooed man they were looking for remained to be seen, but it was the best lead they had so far.

Evan came around the corner, riding a Shire horse with a braided mane. He struggled to lead his horse over to where Budd waited, tugging on the reins with a frustrated sigh.

Budd scoffed and shook his head. "You need to earn a horse's trust, partner. A good mount doesn't have to be ordered around. They know their rider better than most people know their loved ones. Bond with it, and they'll follow."

"He needs some good training is all," Evan replied. "Your horse has a crazy look in its eye."

"This ol' girl and I have been through a lot together." Budd patted Ivory on her side with an affectionate smile. "She's fast and stubborn to a fault, but we have our own way of communicating."

Evan looked skeptical as he tugged his horse over to Budd. He jutted his chin toward the ranch and asked, "How do you want to handle this? If it is Johnny, then he might try to shoot you the second you knock on that door."

"Let me do all the talking," Budd suggested. "It would be best if no one knows who you are. At least we'll have the element of surprise on our side." He headed off down the path that led to the main house of the ranch. Armed guards and farm hands wandered around the land, watching Budd and Evan carefully as they approached the house. The sound of a child's laughter floated out of a window above their heads.

Budd and Evan hitched their horses at a small post near the front porch. It was Budd who knocked, while Evan hung back a bit. Footsteps came from behind the door only a second before it opened.

A man with inky black hair leaned against the doorjamb with a cigar in his right hand and glass in the other. He wore tailored town pants held in place by fine leather suspenders over a paisley vest with a muslin shirt that was tucked in and unbuttoned at the neck. It was clear the man had money—more money than a small cattle ranch could produce during a drought. "What can I do for you, gentlemen?" drawled the well-dressed stranger. Budd could practically see his reflection in the shine of the man's shoes.

"My name is Budd Mansfield. I'm here on behalf of Pratt Dempcy & Company . This here is my partner." Budd gestured over his shoulder at Evan. "We have a couple of questions for Mr. and Mrs. Pepper."

The man straightened to his full height and stepped aside to allow them into the house. "My name is Reginald Pearce, but everyone calls me Reg. Beatrice Pepper is my little sister," said the man. He called out for Beatrice and ushered Budd and Evan into a small sitting room off of the main corridor.

A youthful woman appeared a moment later. She tucked a strand of hair behind her ear and dusted flour off her apron. "Oh! We have guests," she said kindly. "Hello. I'm Beatrice. Welcome to my home."

Budd removed his hat and shook Beatrice's hand gently. Evan followed Budd's lead and shook both Reginald's and Beatrice's hands. The duo sat on a long sofa that sat across from two long-back chairs. A tall man with far more casual clothing than Reginald entered the room. His face was dotted with healing bruises.

"You must be John," Budd said when he felt Evan stiffen beside him. He offered his hand to the newcomer, but John waved a dismissive hand.

"Yes, I'm John Pepper."

Budd noticed how the impolite gesture made Reginald's lip curl in disgust. He cleared his throat and turned his gaze to Beatrice. "Ma'am, I represent a company named Pratt Dempcy & Company. They are a stagecoach company that offers transportation in many states, including here in California."

"How wonderful," she gasped. "But… what does that have to do with us?"

"My job is to ensure safe passage for our patrons and secure their belongings during their travels. Lately, I find myself plagued by a group of bandits that seem to target our stagecoaches specifically," Budd explained. He reached into his satchel and pulled out the drawing of the eagle tattoo. "A witness to one of the recent attacks could describe one bandit. He had the image of an eagle inked onto the inside of his wrist."

Beatrice took the proffered sketch. "I'm sorry, but I do not recognize it," she claimed after only sparing a fleeting glance toward the image. "I sure hope you catch him."

"You see," Budd began, "after the death of one of our drivers, you can imagine we are eager to catch up to the men responsible."

"I'm still not sure what this has to do with us, Mr. Mansfield." Beatrice thrust the sketch back into Budd's hand with a sneer.

"The witness claims a man named Johnny Pepper—"

Beatrice jumped to her feet and placed her hands on her hips. "I dislike your insinuations, sir! That so-called witness must be mistaken. My husband is a good man. He is a loving husband and father who works his fingers to the bone to keep this ranch going."

Budd stood. He lifted his hands in defense as he lowered his voice. "We have to investigate this thoroughly, Mrs. Pepper. A man lost his life in cold blood. If John has nothing to hide, I'm sure he will cooperate with us."

The conversation came to a halt when Beatrice left the room. She stormed into the kitchen with a loud huff. John Pepper sat silently in the chair his wife had vacated. Budd was confused when the man gave no outward sign of worry that he was accused of murder. Evan, on the other hand, had become so tense that he looked like a statue.

Beatrice carried in a tray with an assortment of beverages, but gone was the polite smile she had worn earlier. Her hands trembled slightly as she poured several cups of tea. Budd took the teapot from her hand to keep her from dropping the pristine china. He gave her a reassuring smile and finished serving the beverages as she pulled herself together.

"Now, I know I must have shocked you all with this information, but I really need to get through these questions," Budd said finally. "Mr. Pepper, can you tell me where you were on the morning of September seventh?"

John leaned back in his chair, stroked a pencil-thin goatee, and said, "On the seventh? I reckon I was right here. Probably milking a cow or herding the cattle. There's lots of work to be done here."

Budd sipped his tea slowly, still feeling a twinge of pain at his temples from the night before. "And can anyone on the ranch confirm that? A worker, perhaps?"

"I can," answered Reginald. "John was teaching me a few things. I'm something of an aspiring rancher, myself. And as far as the tattoo is concerned, there was a man in Timber with that same one just the other day. Talk to a barkeep named Bill at the Bull Trotter. He should be able to point you in the right direction."

Budd's stomach turned. There was something about Reginald's helpfulness that rubbed him the wrong way. "Timber? That's several miles away from where the attack took place. Are you sure?"

Reginald's smile grew tense at the corners of his mouth. He cleared his throat and replied, "Now, I can't speak on behalf of bandits, Mr. Mansfield, but if I was running from the law, I would want to get as far away from where the crime happened as I could."

Budd wanted to push Reginald further, but he tried his best to remain focused on John Pepper. "Would you mind rolling back your sleeves for me? Like I said, we have to be thorough."

John Pepper scoffed as he yanked up his sleeves. Both of the man's arms were covered in bandages from wrist to elbow. "There was a storm that rolled through these parts not too long ago," he claimed. "I was badly burned trying to put out the fire started by the lightning. Infections have slowed the healing down. Lost six cattle in that storm."

Budd glanced over at Evan and saw the barely restrained rage that simmered beneath the surface of his calm exterior. However, Evan's curt nod confirmed a storm had rolled through while Budd had been out of town. Though it would have explained the bandages, Budd thought it had been awfully convenient that John's hands hadn't gotten burned while it covered his forearms in bandages. It seemed a strange place to be burned.

"Lightning storms and helpful barkeeps in Timber?" Budd chuckled. "I don't know if you're the most unlucky man in Sacramento or if the stars have aligned themselves in your favor, but that's one heck of a story." He climbed to his feet, signalling Evan to do the same, and set down his teacup. Budd tipped his hat to the Pepper family. "Thank you for your time and hospitality," he said. "If I have any more questions, I will ride back this way. Enjoy the rest of your day, folks."

They strolled back toward the door and took their leave. Evan hopped onto his horse with a white-knuckled grip on the saddle horn. He tore off down the path before Budd could utter a single word. It spoke volumes of the man's character that he had shown such restraint in the face of his enemy.

Chapter 7

Johnny fidgeted in his seat as Rip watched through a gap in the curtains as Budd Mansfield and his partner rode off the property. An uncomfortable silence settled within the room.

Beatrice slammed her teacup onto the side table and stood over her husband, finger pointed at the center of his chest. "You fool!" she screeched. "It ain't like we didn't already have the law breathing down our necks. Now we have the stagecoach company sending their own men! Ripley told you to take care of the man who saw you rob that coach. I suggest you do as he says and do it quick!" Beatrice dropped her hand and visibly struggled to regain her composure.

Johnny took his wife by the hand and pressed a kiss to her knuckles. "I'm gonna handle it, all right? My family is my top priority. He gave Beatrice one of his charming smiles, but she snatched her hand out of his grasp. Johnny stood in the center of the room with his jaw slack as his wife stormed out of the room. The door to the kitchen slammed behind her, leaving no opportunity for further discussion.

Rip kept his back to Johnny, glaring out the window as Mansfield and his partner finally faded into the distance. Johnny wasn't waiting around to get beaten again, so he left through the front door. He felt Rip's eyes burning into him as he walked over to the old barn on the property. The gang all stood up with their guns drawn when he pushed through the doors.

"Y'all are almost as paranoid as Ripley," Johnny said. "Put those things away before one of you accidentally shoots me."

"If I shot you," Hector said, "it wouldn't be an accident."

Johnny rolled his eyes and picked up a lever action rifle and a small pistol from the table that sat against the wall. He shoved some ammunition into the pouch tied to his belt, wandered over to the stable for his horse, and headed into town before the others could distract him with cards and drinking. There was a point he needed to make to Beatrice and Rip. He knew they looked down on him. Most of the time, they treated him like some ill-bred buffoon, still green around the collar. But Johnny had been running with gangs long before the likes of Ripley Eagleson came into his life.

A flash of lightning zipped along the gray-black clouds before a rumble of thunder. Johnny kept a firm grip on the reins and steered his mount away from the path Budd Mansfield had taken. Instead of taking the main road into town, Johnny eased onto a beaten path that led over to the lumberyard. There was no doubt in his mind that it had been Cornwall who ratted him out. Johnny had recognized the burly man just as easily as Cornwall had recognized him.

It had been a fool's hope, thinking Cornwall was smart enough to keep quiet, but Johnny knew now that it had been a mistake allowing the man to live. Cornwall must have started working for the stagecoach company around the time the bank cut their wages. It was just Johnny's rotten luck Cornwall was working the day they robbed that coach. He muttered irritably to himself as he rode to the former bank teller's residence. There was a light in the upstairs bedchamber, which meant Cornwall's wife was home.

Johnny hitched his mount to a nearby tree before he approached the house. He took cover to the left of the door and knocked. Footfalls echoed inside.

A sleepy-eyed woman held a shotgun in her hand as she opened the door. "Who goes there?" she called, but Johnny gave no answer.

He held his breath as she stepped outside to investigate. When she lowered the gun, Johnny grabbed her. He slammed her against the wall, knocking her unconscious.

The shotgun clattered to the floor. Johnny looked around to see if anyone had heard the commotion. When all was silent, he dragged Mrs. Cornwall's limp body inside the house and hogtied her next to the fireplace. He used his bandana as a gag in case she woke before her husband arrived, shoving it between her teeth before he tied it at the base of her skull. The storm outside picked up. Windows rattled, and Johnny went to shut the front door to keep out the rain.

He checked the watch in his pocket. Bernard Cornwall was a creature of habit who arrived home every day at the same time. Everyone in Sacramento was predictable to a fault. Johnny prided himself on being the wild card of the gang. He situated himself on the sofa and watched his pocket watch tick until fifteen minutes after three o'clock arrived. Keys jangled outside the front door right on time.

"Lisa?" called the cheerful man as he hung his waterlogged jacket on the hook near the entrance. "I have been lookin' forward to your cookin' all day. I hope it's somethin' tasty—" Cornwall turned toward the room and stopped dead in his tracks. His eyes widened at the sight of his unconscious wife.

Johnny smiled and flipped his gun out of its holster before Cornwall took another step. "Evenin', Bernard," Johnny chuckled. "A little bird told me you've had my name running out of your mouth lately."

"P-please."

"When I saw you on that wagon, I thought you were a passenger," he said, ignoring Cornwall's plea.

"I rarely work security." Cornwall trembled in his boots, his eyes never wavering from the gun aimed at his chest. "I help manage the office here in Sacramento. We're short on workers lately, so th-they asked me to ride along that day."

"And you told them it was me?"

"N-no!" Cornwall stammered. "I told them that the tattoo—"

Johnny pushed off the couch and moved to stand in front of the other man. He adjusted his aim so his gun pointed down at Lisa Cornwall. "I don't want to hurt anybody. Just tell me where you keep the ledger."

"What ledger?"

"The ledger that Pratt Dempcy & Company has you use to keep track of transports, cargo, and which guns are riding with the stagecoaches," he hissed. Johnny pulled back on the hammer and watched as desperation joined the fear he saw in Cornwall's expression. "And I want it. Now."

***

Timber, California

Budd scraped the last of the muck out of the horseshoes and patted his horse on the side. Stable workers had their place, but Budd reckoned nothing strengthened the bond between a horse and its rider than some good old-fashioned grooming. He paid for a stall at the stables and met with Evan outside the Bull Trotter. The last time Budd had wandered into that saloon, there had been a brawl that landed him in jail for the night. He had hit rock bottom by the time dawn cast shadows over the small town, and he vowed never to let it happen again. Less than a week later, he had accepted the job with Pratt Dempcy & Company.

Evan flicked his cigarette into the road. Smoke bellowed out of his nose as he glared over at the swinging doors. "You sure you want to chase this blind lead?" he asked. "Ripley is just as dirty as his brother-in-law, maybe even dirtier."

"That so?"

"Yep," Evan retorted. "Never seen him do anything wrong… It's just a feeling I get."

"If Ripley is that Reginald feller, I think I know what you mean." Budd scratched at the stubble on his chin. He hadn't gotten a lick of sleep since they left John Pepper's little ranch two days ago. "He rubbed me the wrong way. Too polite under the circumstances. I flat out accused Johnny of murder right in front of him, and he barely said a word."

"From what I hear, Johnny's always on Ripley's bad side. Then again, that trigger-happy lunatic could sour anybody's mood," Evan said with a snort.

Budd held open one of the swinging doors for his partner. Evan walked in front of him as they made their way over to the bar. Inside, it was nearly empty. Only a few day drinkers sat at the round tables with beer bottles clutched in their dirty fingers. Budd brushed a couple of crumbs off the stool before he sat down.

The barkeep eyed him suspiciously and grumbled, "What can I get ya?"

"I'm looking for a man who works here. His name is Bill," Budd said. "Know him?"

"I'm Bill."

Evan's hand lowered to his gun belt as he turned his back to Budd and the barkeep.

Budd nodded. He slid a dollar across the bar. "I'll take whatever that'll get me."

"You boys look familiar," Bill replied. "Have we met?"

Budd watched the man's hands as he poured dark amber liquid into a foggy glass. The heat caused droplets of water to appear along the rim. "Listen, partner," he said with a low rumble in his chest. "I'm sure they have paid you a pretty penny to send me running around in circles if I started asking questions. So I won't take up too much of your time."

Bill stashed the bottle on a tall shelf and gripped the edge of the bar. His big bushy brow furrowed, and his yellowed teeth flashed as he spoke. "You must be Mansfield."

"Why don't we skip the pleasantries, huh? And you can tell me all about your buddy John Pepper and his brother

Ripley," Budd suggested. "Make it worth the three-day trip it took to get here, and I might not tell the sheriff of this miserable town that you've got some rather unusual things going on behind that iron door around back."

Bill swallowed noisily and took a big swig of an open beer beside him. He dabbed away the sweat from his neck before he met Budd's eye. "All I know is Ripley pays me to keep folks from hassling John," the man said nervously. "Rip is a good man trying to do right by his family. Takes real good care of those in his employment, but—"

"But Johnny's the wayward little brother-in-law?"

Bill nodded. He lowered his voice to a barely there whisper. "People are terrified of John. He's unstable."

"What about Rip? What can you tell me about him?" Budd asked. "Seems he showed up out of the blue."

"I have nothin' to say about Rip." Bill used the filthy rag in his hand to wipe down the bar. "Tell the sheriff there's something foul goin' on out back. I don't care. I ain't tellin' you nothin' about Rip."

"Eagleson seems to have some very loyal friends," Budd muttered as he lifted his glass to take a sip. The drink was bitter on his tongue and tasted like fire. "Let's get back to Johnny, then. Shall we?"

Evan waited until the other men at the bar moved over to the card table and then slid over to the seat beside Budd. The two of them made quite an intimidating pair, Budd reckoned.

He gestured to the tattoo of an eagle on the back of Bill's hand that was like the one the witness had seen. "Somebody talked, Bill," Budd said. "They saw a mark like that on

Johnny. Now, you don't strike me as a man who is comfortable with blood on his hands, but you just might end up with soiled palms if that witness gets silenced. Can you live with yourself?"

The barkeep was quiet for a moment. Bill chewed on his bottom lip and picked at the loose threads on his rag. He leaned over the bar between Budd and Evan. "A couple of Johnny's friends were runnin' their mouths in here one night. They had a few too many beers and started sayin' how Johnny killed a stagecoach driver."

"Would you be willing to say that in front of a judge?"

Chapter 8

Sheriff Dawson sat with his head in his hands as Budd explained the latest development in his investigation. Bill had agreed to testify against John Pepper if Budd and Evan brought him in on murder charges. The problem Budd currently faced was convincing the sheriff to lift the ban on Evan.

"I told you I didn't want Evan Farris anywhere near this case," the sheriff grumbled. "He's a criminal, Mr. Mansfield."

"I wouldn't have known where to find John Pepper without him." Budd paced in front of the lawman's desk. "He's headed over to the witness's house right now. If we get Mr. Cornwall and his wife to back Bill's statement—"

"Cornwall?" Sheriff Dawson asked hastily. "Budd, they killed Bernard Cornwall."

Time seemed to hold still for a second. Budd plopped gracelessly into a nearby chair. "How'd it happen?"

"Shot."

"And his wife?" Budd croaked. His throat felt tight and uncomfortable, barely able to get the words out.

"She was shot too. By the grace of God, Lisa Cornwall is alive, but the doctor says he's unsure when she'll wake." Sheriff Dawson picked up a pen from his desk and wrote something down. "Under normal circumstances, I wouldn't even consider hiring a man like Evan Farris.... but if you truly believe he is an asset in this investigation, I will allow him to assist you."

Budd reached out to grab the note, but the sheriff snatched it back for a moment.

"Don't make me regret this," he said. "Farris's mistakes are yours. You are accountable for his actions."

"You have my word." Budd reached for the note again, and the sheriff handed it over. He took his leave as he struggled to digest the news of Bernard Cornwall's death. Ripley and John had gotten exactly what they wanted. The trip to Timber made sure Budd was out of the way long enough for their wicked plans to unfold. Bernard Cornwall's death was on him, not Bill. And their only hope of catching John Pepper had died with the witness.

Budd took his time as he walked over to the hotel. All the rooms at the inn had been rented already, so he had reserved his old room at the hotel before he went and talked with the sheriff. He shuffled up to the room with his eyes trained on the floor. Evan had made it back before Budd. They almost bumped into one another as Evan hobbled drunkenly over to the bed.

Budd closed the door. He took one look at the bottle in Evan's hand and felt a familiar twinge of sadness. "I take it you heard what happened," Budd said, peeling off his jacket.

"What gave it away?"

"It's not even noon, and you're already full as a tick." He grabbed the beer from Evan's hand before it crashed to the floor. Budd cursed under his breath and set it down on the dresser. "Don't put this on yourself, Evan."

"We knew it was a ploy," Evan replied. "We knew what they were up to, and we went anyway just because Sheriff Dawson wanted things by the book."

Budd tucked the note from the sheriff into Evan's hand. "This ain't on the sheriff, either. We were chasing a lead."

"Because of us, John Pepper has torn another family apart. How many people need to die before he's locked away?" Evan sat up and unfolded the paper. He scoffed as he read the sheriff's offer, balled the note up, and tossed it across the room. "Temporary immunity in Sacramento under the condition of full cooperation with the law, huh? That's the best he could do? I guess I'm just tired. So tired of all of it."

Budd knew better than most people what Evan meant. He had shouldered his fair share of blame, carried the weight of burdens, and held grudges for longer than any man ever should. "With the sheriff's blessing, you'll be able to help more with bringing down Johnny," Budd said. "You still have to stay away from the stagecoaches. In the meantime, however, I need to find out more about the ace of spades left on the attacked coaches and find where the rest of the gang is hiding."

"The Old Mill."

"Huh?" Budd turned to look at Evan. "You think the gang would hide out at an old mill?"

"Not an old mill," his friend chuckled. "The Old Mill. A sharp businessman from Chicago came to the region about seven years ago. He tried to build a steel mill, but bandits ran him out of the state before it was finished. Locals called the abandoned building site the Old Mill."

"All right, but why would they be holed up there?" Budd kicked his boots off and unfolded his bedroll at the foot of the bed.

"It's practically a fortress," Evan explained. "The stone walls are strong and tall, and there's not a lot of windows to cover, which means they're protected from any incoming attacks."

Budd let loose a few colorful curse words. He swallowed down the rest of his profanity with a drink of water straight from the pitcher beside the bed. "No way we'll be able to get close enough to arrest the culprits. Best we stick to finding a plan to catch them in the act."

Only a soft snore followed Budd's words.

He set the pitcher of water on the bedside table and pulled the covers over Evan, who had passed out on the mattress. The floorboards creaked in protest beneath his weight as he lowered himself to the floor. Budd groaned quietly. He felt an ache in his muscles as he settled onto the floor, allowing the tension to leave his body. Daylight still poured through the shutters, but it only took a few minutes for Budd to fall asleep. He tossed and turned, troubled by the tragic fate that had befallen the Cornwall family.

***

Rip waited until nightfall and then walked up a set of stairs behind the general store. He knocked on a door that hung on loose hinges, listening for the sound of approaching footfalls. The door cracked open with a squeak.

Sadey Conner's beautiful pale face came into sight. Cat-like green eyes gazed at Rip through a mane of wild, golden curls. "Rip?"

"Good evening, Miss Conner," Rip drawled as his eyes lazily appreciated the soft, feminine features of the woman who stood before him. But many men had fallen victim to her feminine wiles in the past, and Rip was determined not to be one of them. Sadey Conner had the beauty of a well-bred heiress and the lethal skill of a trained killer. "I need your services."

Sadey opened the door further and pulled on a thin robe. She pushed her hair out of her face, glancing at Rip in confusion. "I'm retired."

"Not from what I hear."

"Then you heard wrong," she retorted sharply. "I'm doin' what's right now."

Rip shook his head before he reached out to place his hand on her shoulder. Sadey flinched, but she didn't pull away. "You owe me, Sadey Ann," he growled with a sinister smile. "I saved your life when that U.S. Marshal nearly shot you dead, remember? Now I'm looking to cash in on that debt."

"Rip… I came to Sacramento for a fresh start," Sadey said quietly. "If I break the law here, then I'll have to move again, and the government is still lookin' for me."

"Just do this for me. One last job, I promise." He dropped his hand to his side. Rip held her stare as if she were his equal, which was more respect than most men would have shown her. "I need you to get rid of Budd Mansfield. Quietly.

Take him out and then leave town. Send word when it's done, and I'll wire you money."

"Cash," she demanded. "In advance or no dice, Rip. I'm not one of the boys in your gang. I know you don't send the money from the stagecoach robberies to their families."

Rip clenched his jaw and counted to ten silently in his head before he spoke. "I'll give you my word—"

"It ain't good enough," Sadey chuckled. "I've known you for a long time—since I was a little girl—and I know you'll have me killed after you get what you want. I'd rather do the job and then go my own way. For real this time. Far away where you'll never find me."

He took two steps toward her and leaned in close to her ear. "I'll always find you, little Sadey Ann." Rip lowered his voice to a whisper and said, "There is nowhere in this great big wild west where you can hide. Run from your past all you want, but you can never run from me. We are birds of a feather, you and I."

Sadey brazenly shoved against Rip's chest, causing him to stumble backward. She pinned him with a seething glare. "No more games. I want the money now, and that's that."

"One hundred."

"Five."

"Two."

"Four."

"Three hundred dollars and a train ticket east," Rip negotiated. "That's my last offer. Take it, or I walk out of here without giving you a dime." He reached into his pocket and pulled out a bundle of cash.

Sadey's eyes were riveted to the money as he made a show of counting it. "Fine."

"Cash now," he said as he handed over three hundred dollars. "Train ticket after the job is done. Send a message to the ranch, and I'll meet you at the train station." Rip turned his back to Sadey and walked back toward the door. His hand touched the doorknob just as her quiet voice broke the silence.

"Budd Mansfield... that the same one who used to work for the Pinkertons?"

Rip's heart plummeted. "What?" he asked.

"A man named Budd Mansfield shot and killed a former associate of mine," she said. "He worked for the agency... Well, not really. Mansfield was the guy those Pinkertons called when they wanted to work outside the law."

The tall, muscular man who questioned Johnny at the ranch had seemed like more than a security manager for a stagecoach company. Budd Mansfield was the sort of man who would make most hardened bounty hunters quake in their boots.

Rip faced Sadey once more with his hand still on the doorknob. "He's working for Pratt Dempcy & Company. Security mostly, but he recently started poking around my operation."

"Then it's good you want him dead," Sadey snickered. "Pinkertons weren't happy when he left. They want their huntin' dog back." She walked up to Rip and pulled his hand away from the door. "Did Johnny have anythin' to do with that local man's death?"

"You know I can't talk to you about what happens in the gang."

"He did, didn't he? I can see the truth in your eyes. Johnny killed that man."

Rip looked away from Sadey's prying gaze. He couldn't stand the disgust he saw in their depths. "Business was taken care of. Loose ends tied up."

"Then you best hope I kill Budd Mansfield before he finds out who you really are." Sadey's expression became grim. She snatched her hand away from Rip and moved deeper into the room.

Rip considered Sadey's warning for a moment.

The Pinkertons had had him in their sights for a long time. Each of their attempts to catch him ended with a lot of unnecessary deaths. If Budd Mansfield really was the man Sadey described, then Rip reckoned this time around would end the same.

"I find myself fascinated by the prospect," he replied. "For the first time in many years, I feel like there might be something to look forward to."

Chapter 9

Sweat collected along the curve of Budd's spine as he lay in the dark. Something shifted in the atmosphere, and suddenly the scent of soap clung to the musty summer air. He reached beneath his pillow for his knife and focused on steadying his breathing. His eyes remained shut. Soundless footsteps shifted the floorboards where he rested.

A shadow fell over Budd, cutting through the ray of moonlight that had cast a ghostly glow over his sharp features. He struck with the speed of a puma, slashing his knife in a deadly arc. The intruder knocked the blade out of his hand, and it went clattering to the floor.

Budd's eyes flew open. Even in the darkened room, he could tell Evan was no longer in bed. Budd swung his fist blindly. The intruder stomped on his chest, squeezing every bit of air out of his lungs. He shoved the boot away and rolled to the side. Budd jumped to his feet. He grabbed onto the shadowy figure when it went to hit him again. Soft curves took him by surprise. The intruder was more than a head shorter than him and almost as light as a bag of flour. There was no doubt in his mind that his would-be murderer was a woman.

"Stop struggling!" he barked in her ear.

She threw her weight to the floor, knocking him off balance. Budd tripped over his discarded boots and landed beside his knife. He gripped the hilt with sweaty fingers before he lunged at the woman. She stepped to the left at the last minute, and Budd's momentum sent him careening into the wardrobe. He recovered quickly and swept his leg beneath her. She toppled over. Budd pinned her legs to the floor with his knees and felt the sting of a knife against his throat.

"I wouldn't do that if I were you," he snarled. Budd glanced down at her belly, where his own knife hovered. "Make any sudden moves, and we both die. Right here. Right now."

The door to the room swung open. Evan stood at the threshold with his gun raised. Lamps in the corridor bathed the room in light, giving him a good look at her face for the first time. Budd saw a flicker of interest in her gaze. Though she was one of the most beautiful women he had ever seen... his heart belonged to another. Still, Budd had the idea to use her interest in his favor.

"Put the knife down," Evan ordered.

The woman did as she was told, letting the curved dagger slip from her hands. The weapon was old-fashioned for his taste. Evan kicked it out of her reach as Budd pulled himself to his feet. He shared a puzzled look with his partner. Evan forced the woman into a chair and secured her arms behind her back with a length of rope from Budd's bag.

"What's your name?" Budd asked.

"Beth."

"Her name is Sadey Conner," Evan corrected. He glared at the mysterious woman, and Budd assumed it was a silent warning not to lie again. "She's new in town. Only been here a few months. Works on Tom Well's farm in the scullery."

Budd kneeled in front of Sadey Conner. He looked straight into her eyes and asked, "Who hired you to kill me?"

"Who said they paid me?" she snickered. "You've got enemies, Mr. Mansfield. A long list of folks wantin' you dead up north, from what I hear."

His stomach did flips. Nausea stained the back of his tongue with the taste of bile. "You know me?"

"Only through the stories. Did me a favor killin' Denis O'Malley."

The name was familiar, but Budd had made it a habit not to ask too many questions when the Pinkertons sent him after somebody. "I'll ask you one more time," he replied. "Who hired you to kill me?"

Sadey Conner's eyes grew cold. She clenched her jaw and remained silent.

"Look, I ain't going to hurt you, Sadey. I just want to get justice for the folks who have been hurt by some bad people." Budd pushed his hair out of his face. He knew he was a handsome man, well above average if the suggestive glances around town were anything to go by.

Sadey watched his movements. Her eyes darted down to his scarred hands and then back up to his face. A pink flush stole across her cheeks, and Budd smiled. "You ain't no better than they are," she said finally. "You're a killer. Only difference between you and them is you're a trained mutt workin' for the law."

"Did Ripley Eagleson hire you to kill me?" Budd muttered.

Sadey's mouth snapped shut. She trembled with rage.

But Budd knew he had her in the palm of his hand. He felt her attraction to him like a burning fire. Miss Conner must not have been used to being beaten at her own games. Budd was amused, even as he remained focused on his goal. Any other man would have been seduced and killed before dawn, he reckoned. "When is the next attack?"

"I don't know." Sadey shrugged.

"You know something," Evan hissed from the corner of the room. He moved to stand behind Sadey and loomed over her threateningly.

Budd brought her attention back to him with a snap of his fingers. "I get the feeling you could have killed me if you wanted to. It would have been a quick job—in and out before anybody was the wiser. But you hesitated." He tilted her head up with the tip of his finger and forced her to meet his stare once more. "You've got a heart, Sadey."

Tears welled in her big green eyes. "I c-can't tell you."

"More people will get hurt if you stay silent," he mumbled. "Whatever your employer is holding over you... whatever you're running from... this is your chance for redemption. Tell me when the next attack is, and I'll do my best to help you."

"No one can help me."

"Then tell me because it's the right thing to do," Budd implored. He shifted closer to Sadey and watched as her eyelids grew heavy with desire. "Talk to me, Sadey."

She opened her mouth but forced her eyes to the ground at the last minute. Sadey sighed like a woman with a heavy heart. "It don't matter what you do. He knows all of your tricks. Even if you clap me in irons and drag me down to the sheriff, it won't change a thing. Nobody can catch the gang behind all this... not even you."

***

Three days passed without a single lead. Budd and Evan were going stir crazy, holed up in their room at the inn with little to distract them. Sheriff Dawson stopped by just long enough to let them know John Pepper had left town. That was as far as their investigation had panned out so far. Budd knew in his gut that John had gone to Old Mill, where Evan believed the rest of the gang was hiding out.

"You should talk to Mr. Thayer," Evan said for the hundredth time that morning. "Maybe he can get—"

"Mr. Thayer will need more than our word that John Pepper was the one who killed Mr. Cornwall and the driver." Budd paced across the floor and scratched at the stubble on his chin. "And Dawson says his hands are tied until we find something that proves Rip and John are linked to the gang behind the attacks."

Out of the corner of his eye, Budd saw Sadey Conner fidget in the chair Evan had tied her to. They kept her fed and bathed. Budd often untied her from the chair so she could sleep in the bed, and he even gave her privacy to relieve herself in the outhouse when she needed. Despite all his attempts at kindness, she still hadn't offered up any more information. Sadey simply sat quietly with her eyes trained on Budd with each passing minute.

When noon arrived that day, Evan's restlessness finally won the battle. He picked up his hat and disappeared through the door without a word of where he was headed. Budd saw it as his opportunity to talk with Sadey in private. His mind turned to the events that had followed the death of the driver. Cornwall's untimely end seemed like a desperate attempt to cover the gang's tracks, in his opinion.

"We should talk now we're alone," Budd began. "Why would your employer want me dead?"

"You talk too much, Mr. Mansfield. Askin' around town about the killin'." Sadey shook her head, but a slight smile tugged at the corners of her mouth. "You were bound to get some unwanted attention."

"My work with the Pinkerton Detective Agency was all off the books. I never once met the agents who hired me for my services," Budd explained. "I provided information and, when it was needed, protected their investments."

"Was Denis an investment?"

"No. He tried robbing the train we were using to transport prisoners to their trial," he replied. "He used violence to threaten us, and we responded in kind."

Sadey blew a strand of her hair out of her face, but it fell against her eyelashes.

Budd shuffled over, tucked the curl behind her ear, and cupped her cheek gently. "I've done a lot of bad things, Sadey," he continued as he gazed into her eyes. "But I'm not an evil man. I can help you if you would be willing to help me."

She licked her dry, slightly cracked lips and nodded. "I'll tell you everythin' I know... but you have to promise you'll get me out of this blasted city and far away from the likes of Rip Eagleson and that crazy brother of his."

Budd released Sadey. He pulled the knife from his belt and cut through the ropes that held her captive. Sadey rubbed her wrists. Budd winced when he saw how raw her delicate skin had become. He pulled her over to the washbasin before pressing a damp rag to the reddened skin. Part of him knew there was a possibility no one had ever shown her such compassion.

Budd and Sadey sat down on the edge of the bed. She told Budd that Johnny got hold of a ledger that belonged to Cornwall, a ledger containing everything the gang needed to put Pratt Dempcy & Company out of business.

Budd cursed and then muttered an apology. He was filled with an anger he thought he had buried a long time ago. All of his plans to keep the stagecoaches safe were compromised. Cornwall hadn't worked with the company long, but he had written down just enough of the details for Budd to panic.

"Help us catch John Pepper, and I promise to get you as far east as I can," he replied. "I don't have family and not much in the way of friends, but I have someone in Philadelphia who can help you start over."

"And you won't turn me over to the law?" The confidence in Sadey's smile faltered. For a split second, Budd saw true vulnerability in her expression.

He responded with a shake of his head. Though there was a time when he would have done anything to put a mercenary behind bars, Budd was a man of his word. He stood up and walked over to the door. "You can have this room for yourself tonight. Evan and I will bunk in the room just across the hall."

"Budd—" Sadey reached out for him but stopped before her hand brushed his arm.

"Yes?"

"The person in Philadelphia... Who are they?" she asked. "I mean, can they be trusted?"

"Her name is Rose Buchanan." Budd's heart stuttered just at the mention of her name. He grinned from ear to ear and said, "From the moment I first laid eyes on Rose, I knew there was no one else for me. She means the world to me, and I hope one day she will do me the honor of being my wife."

The last of the mischief and desire that danced in Sadey's eyes vanished. "Oh..." she stammered. A pale hand lifted to touch the thin silver chain around her neck.

"Sadey, I'm—"

"I like you," she said, cutting Budd off before he could finish his explanation. "Perhaps I was simply hopeful you might fancy me a little. Silly of me, really."

Chapter 10

Iron Stallion Saloon

Sacramento

"If Johnny is anything like he was when we were growing up, he's still got a weakness for beautiful women," Evan said as Budd clicked their beers together in an unspoken toast. Their table overlooked the main room of the saloon, giving them a perfect view of the entrance. Sadey Conner sauntered over to the table with a sultry grin.

Budd tipped his hat to her as she set down two plates of lamb and potatoes. "Ma'am," he said, as if they had never met.

Sadey had agreed to help them trap John Pepper in exchange for her freedom and the chance at a new life. Without her help, Budd and Evan would have had no choice but to storm the gates of the Old Mill on their own. Budd disliked the idea of walking into a bandit hideout without somebody to back him up, but Pratt Dempcy & Company couldn't spare any of their men. So, for now, at least, the three of them were on their own.

"I've seen that man in here with John before," Evan muttered a few moments later. He made a subtle gesture to a man at the bar wearing a serape and picked up his fork. "His name is Hector Vasquez. He keeps an eye on Johnny for Rip. If he's here…"

"Then John Pepper ain't too far behind," Budd said as realization dawned. He took a sip from his bottle and watched Sadey out of the corner of his eye. They had waited long enough for a shot at their target. Sadey just had to get John Pepper alone and give the signal. The rest was up to Budd and Evan.

"You think we can trust her?"

Budd looked over at Evan and shrugged. "Whether she tips him off or upholds her end of the bargain, we've got a chance to catch him before he goes back to the Old Mill," he replied. "Getting him in the room or getting him on the road makes no difference to me."

"He's slippery."

"Yeah, well, so are we." Budd adjusted the brim of his hat and leaned back in his chair. He gave off an air of relaxation, though he was anything but relaxed. Anxiousness and worry tangled together in the pit of his stomach.

The saloon smelled of meat, sweat, and liquor. Boots scuffed along the sticky floorboards as patrons drunkenly danced around the tables. Budd's gaze flickered over every face, memorizing each one in case he had to ask questions later. The crowd looked like ordinary folks at first glance. But as Budd took a closer look, he saw some burly thugs seated at the tables.

Hector Vasquez moved to the left of one of the rough-looking strangers before he leaned in to whisper something. Budd stiffened in his seat. His ears strained to pick up the conversation, but the task proved impossible with the piano playing. Sadey caught Budd's eye and placed herself at the stranger's back.

When the men separated, Sadey disappeared behind the bar and the wall of men trying to get a drink. Budd waited with a headache throbbing at his temples. He held his breath until Sadey reappeared. She kept a smile pasted on her face as she carried a tray full of drinks over to Budd and Evan's table. Trembling fingers lowered a glass of bourbon onto the table, and Budd saw a note tucked under the glass.

He opened his mouth to speak, but Sadey was gone in the blink of an eye. Budd slipped the note from beneath the bourbon. Feminine writing flowed across the scrap of paper. Budd bit down on the inside of his cheek to keep from cursing as he read Sadey's note. Take care of the big guys. I'll handle John when he gets here. Room 4.

"Think you can cause a scene?" Budd asked Evan.

A slow, cunning smile appeared on his partner's face. The former outlaw stood up with a clatter and hobbled over to the piano with a beer clutched in his hand. Budd heard a loud commotion a minute later, and they tossed Evan over the bar. Hector and the stranger grabbed Evan by the back of his shirt and dragged him out of sight.

Budd waited a few seconds before he followed them. He kept his head down, walking along a small corridor that led to the kitchen and the back entrance. Light flickered beneath the doors as he passed, casting a grim light on his pinched expression. Budd squeezed his hands into fists and strained to hear the muffled voices just outside.

Hector Vasquez's wide shoulders shrouded Evan in shadow. The long dark braid that dangled along his spine swayed as the outlaw shouted at Budd's partner in Spanish. Budd could only make out a few of the words. Vasquez's thin mustache curled up as he pulled his lips back in a snarl, just before he slammed his fist into Evan's jaw.

The door burst open and startled the outlaws. Budd reached for his gun, but Vasquez's friend knocked it out of his hand. A shoulder slammed into Budd's middle, and he toppled over. Evan leaped to his feet before he threw himself onto the outlaw's back. Vasquez whirled around. Budd ducked just in time to avoid the meaty fist that flew right toward his face. His step faltered, but he used the momentum to knock the second outlaw onto his back.

Evan let out a hiss of air as the burly outlaw nearly crushed him. He rolled to the left and picked Budd's pistol up from the ground. Evan pulled the trigger, but nothing happened. He slapped the side of the barrel and attempted to remove the dirt that was stuffed inside the chamber. "It's jammed!" he groaned right as Vasquez kicked him square in the center of his chest.

Budd winced when Evan hit the ground.

"You picked the wrong night to start a fight," Vasquez snapped and smashed his fist into the side of Budd's head, causing him to stumble as spots danced in his vision.

Budd's back hit the wall. He shook his head, but it only made his stomach heave. Vasquez prepared for another punch, but Budd fought past his nausea and jumped to the side. His boot hit a shovel that had been leaning against the wall. He dropped and swept it up before it fell into the dirt. With a wide swing, Budd brought the shovel down onto Vasquez's back. The outlaw crumpled.

"You hit like a lady," Evan spat. Blood trickled from between his lips before he wiped it up with his sleeve. "I've had worse beatings from my nana."

Budd rolled his eyes at Evan's goading. He tossed the shovel aside, giving Vasquez the opportunity to run before things got ugly. Unfortunately, the outlaw was a touch too stupid to take the hint and jabbed his fist into Budd's stomach. Budd reared his arm back, only to get knocked off his feet. The second outlaw had tossed Evan right at Budd.

Vasquez grabbed onto a handful of dirt and tossed it into Budd's eyes as he attempted to stand up, but Evan sprung to his feet, grabbed Vasquez's revolver from the holster at his right hip, and aimed the gun at the other outlaw. The two criminals spoke in a flurry of Spanish that neither Budd nor Evan understood, but the look of fear in Vasquez's eyes told them everything they needed to know.

Budd blinked furiously, trying to clear his vision. "You called him your brother," he said. "The men in your gang must be as close as family can get without being blood relatives. It would be a shame if you returned to your boss one man short."

"Boss?"

"Ripley Eagleson," Evan growled. "We know you two are in his gang."

"I don't know what you are talkin' about, gringo."

"Play dumb all you want, but we know the truth," Budd grumbled as he circled the two men. "I'll give you until the count of five to get out of here. And trust me when I say this will be the only time you walk away from me, a free man."

Vasquez tossed his head back and laughed like a maniac. "I don't know who you are… but you… you are a very funny man."

"This ain't a laughing matter, friend." The darkness in Budd's eyes made the outlaws pause. "And you don't need to know my name to comprehend I'm not the sort of man who makes threats without following them through."

Vasquez and the other outlaw shared a look as Budd began the countdown. Evan cocked the hammer of the revolver and tilted his head to the side.

"You'll regret this, gringo," Vasquez gulped. "No one messes with us. I suggest you sleep with your eyes open." He gestured to the other outlaw and then slowly backed out of the alley between the saloon and the barbershop.

When they were out of sight, Budd grabbed Evan by the arm and steered him up the stairs that led to the second floor of the saloon. "Sadey said Johnny's in room four, and we've wasted enough time already," he said as he panted for air.

Five or six girls giggled to themselves on the other side of the door. Budd tongued the cut on his lip and knocked twice. A red-haired woman with wine-stained lips and dark makeup around her eyes popped open the lock. Budd stepped inside, choking on a plume of smoke that clogged the air in the upper lounge.

The woman batted her eyelashes as she gazed at him with an appraising look. "Want some company, handsome?" she drawled.

"Actually, I'm looking for room four. My partner and I are supposed to be meeting an old friend." Budd smiled widely, even as he felt slightly ill at the prospect of any woman's company who wasn't his Rose.

The painted lady pointed at a door near to where they stood.

He tasted blood from his busted lip and glanced down the corridor. "Thank you, ma'am."

"Any time, sweetheart."

Budd took the lead and limped past the women. Evan, on the other hand, gave them a suggestive smolder that caused the red-haired woman to grin from ear to ear. There wasn't a doubt in Budd's mind that Evan would have tried to sweet-talk more information out of the ladies if not for the cutting look from Budd. They were short on time. And the thought of Sadey alone with a madman like John Pepper made Budd's mind venture down a dark path. He approached the door with cautious steps and pressed his ear to the wood. The sound of sloshing water caught him off guard.

"If he's in the bath, he's unarmed," Budd whispered to his partner. "Wait for Sadey's signal."

With a nod, Evan handed Budd the sidearm he had taken from Hector Vasquez, then he retrieved a small knife from his boot. Budd stood on the left side of the door, and Evan stood on the right. They gripped their weapons tightly as Sadey's voice reached Budd's ears.

Chapter 11

"You got a lot of tension in these shoulders. Seems you've had a long day," chuckled Sadey as she scrubbed Johnny's scarred back.

He snorted in reply and watched as the light of the setting sun caused the soap bubbles to sparkle like diamonds. It wasn't safe for him at the ranch, not with Budd Mansfield always one step behind him. Johnny had never felt as if the hangman's noose was dangling over his head before.

And if Budd Mansfield was sniffing around the gang, then Johnny figured the Pinkertons weren't too far behind. According to Rip, Mansfield used to be one of their contractors, and that didn't sit well with Johnny. He got twitchy whenever he felt cornered. If not for his wife and daughter, Johnny would have left Sacramento a long time ago. He belonged out on the trail, deep in unforgiving terrain. Not a day went by that he hadn't missed the smell of the rain and pine and the feel of mud beneath his boots.

"This one looks pretty recent," said Sadey.

Johnny scowled over his arm as her finger gently traced three slashes down his bicep where Cornwall's wife had dug her nails into the muscle. The woman had put up one heck of a fight. "Got it a few days back," he replied. "Racoon was digging a hole in the side of the barn. Had to get him off the land."

"And this one?"

Johnny flinched when she touched the bandage on his neck. Ripley had the temperament of a wolverine whenever Johnny got into trouble. He wrapped his fingers around Sadey's wrist and squeezed. She let out a little gasp that made him smile. "None of your business," Johnny hissed. "Keep your questions to yourself or else I'll toss you out of here."

He watched the muscles in her throat work as she swallowed. Her fear was as sweet to him as a rare wine and far more intoxicating. And yet… there was something familiar about her face. Johnny searched through the depths of his liquor-addled memory, but he failed to come up with a name. She reminded him of a deer with its ears perked up, sensing an unseen hunter among the tall grass of a meadow.

"I meant no offense," she whimpered. Those cherry-red lips trembled slightly as she spoke.

Johnny released her arm. He leaned back against the wall of the tub and closed his eyes while Sadey's delicate hands massaged his shoulders, carefully avoiding the bandage. Johnny let out a small chuckle. "You know," he said, "there have been men, men like my brother-in-law, who believe they've shaped this world into what it is using strength and unity. And then there are men like me, men who know fear and money are the beating heart of humanity. Trust me. Ain't nothing good ever been built without blood."

"I don't trust anyone with a serpent's tongue," the woman said as she reached out of sight. "You, John Pepper, are no man. You're a monster… a killer who—"

Johnny's eyes shot open. He gripped the slippery sides of the tub and tried to stand, but a knife kissed the delicate flesh of his throat. "What's going on here? Who are you?"

"I wouldn't do that if I were you." Warm breath puffed against his cheek as Sadey chuckled. She pressed the knife closer and called out for someone.

Johnny held his breath.

Old iron hinges squeaked loudly as the door opened. Budd Mansfield and his partner appeared with their guns drawn. Grim expressions stretched over their faces. Mansfield's broad shoulders pushed through the open doorway, his large body casting a foreboding shadow over the room. Anger, thick like molasses, filled the air. Johnny stared at the gun aimed at his head as the other man retrieved the discarded pair of trousers from the floor.

"Out of the tub," Mansfield growled. "Nice and slow. Do anything foolish, and I'll be riding out to that ranch of yours to deliver some bad news to your wife and daughter."

Sadey lowered the knife as Johnny stood up. Water cascaded down his back and dripped onto the floor. He lifted his hands up, stepped over the side of the tub, and stood perfectly still. Mansfield's partner threw Johnny's trousers at his chest with a smirk.

Back at the ranch, when he had first met Mansfield and his partner, Johnny had been struck by a sense of guilt he couldn't place. Now, in the faint light cast by the oil lamp, Johnny came face to face with a man he never expected to see alive. "Evan Farris," he breathed. Steam from the bath moistened his skin as he pulled on his trousers. "It's been a long time since we've seen each other."

Evan rushed forward with malice in his gaze. "I'll kill you!"

Budd Mansfield held his partner back with a firm grip on his arm. "He ain't worth it! Don't throw your freedom away for the likes of him, Farris."

"My wife… my child…" Evan groaned. "I have lived in utter agony since you and that pathetic gang destroyed our town. The only thing that has kept me going is the hope that one day I will avenge them."

Johnny was grabbed and thrown into a chair near the bed. Drops of water splattered onto the tattered sheets. Budd Mansfield stood over him, Evan paced across the floor, and Sadey lounged upon the mattress.

She cleaned her nails out with the tip of her knife and smiled at Johnny. "You must have taken one too many blows to the head if you don't recognize me," the woman snickered. "The name is Sadey Conner."

"You're Rip's little pet." A split second after the words left his mouth, Sadey threw her knife. The blade soared through the air and landed just a hair's breadth from Johnny's leg with a thwack. "Are you crazy?"

Budd Mansfield pulled the knife free and held it against Johnny's cheek. "She ain't the one you need to be afraid of. I suggest you talk."

"I got nothing to say," Ripley spat.

"We know that brother-in-law of yours isn't too worried about what happens to you. You'd be lucky if he dropped a single tear at your burial. Do you really want to go down protecting him? Because if we don't catch the rest of your gang, it's you who will take the blame."

Johnny looked up into Budd Mansfield's unwavering gaze and said, "You're already too late, Mr. Mansfield. The gang is on their way to attack another one of them stagecoaches. Cornwall's ledger said an heiress has half a fortune in that strongbox."

Budd leaned against the wall with a gun in his hand and his eyes trained on Evan as he worked over John Pepper. Tiny dots of blood peppered the floor, mixing with the water that still dripped from the outlaw's hair. Budd cocked his head to the side, observed John Pepper's expression, and waited for the exact moment he saw defeat in his enemy's eyes.

"That's enough, Evan," Budd muttered. He left his place at the far wall and circled John Pepper. The outlaw's shoulders slumped forward. Budd grabbed onto Johnny's chin, tilting his head back so he could get a good look at him. New and old bruises painted the man's face in shades of yellow, red, black, and blue. "You look like you're ready to talk."

"East trail," John gurgled. "They're riding along the east trail and cutting off the stagecoach before they reach the valley. Everyone was supposed to meet on the hill's crest at sunset and attack once it was dark. Coach was set to arrive at nine o'clock."

Budd's stomach twisted painfully. It had been nearly six when he and Evan first entered the saloon. He released John long enough to yank him out of the chair. "Sadie, go ahead of us and ready the horses," Budd ordered as he dragged the outlaw toward the door.

Sadey dashed down the hallway through the door that led to the staircase out back and disappeared into the evening light.

John Pepper squirmed like a fish out of water. He kicked his legs and bucked his hips, trying to break free of Budd's white-knuckled grip. Budd slammed John against the corridor wall. The impact knocked the air clean out of the outlaw's lungs. Soiled doves kept their heads low as they hurried down to the bar, leaving the three men alone upstairs.

Silence fell over the hallway as John's feeble resistance ended. Evan moved to stand beside Budd and John. His bruised knuckles cracked as he squeezed his hands into fists. There was a desperation to Evan that Budd understood, but they couldn't afford to lose their heads when they were so close to catching the bandits.

"Want me to knock him out?" Evan asked, dropping his voice to a whisper.

"We need him to lead us to the ambush site. He's no use to us if he's unconscious." Budd shook his head and continued down the hallway.

John Pepper stumbled alongside him, blinking his swollen eyes wildly at Evan as he held open the door for Budd. The sound of a dog barking and drunken laughter met them.

Sadey whistled.

Budd's head whipped around, and he spotted the horses on the road. Once they wrestled John onto the back of Evan's horse, Budd tied the outlaw's hands with the same rope that had once held Sadey captive. Folks stopped to take a gander at the sight, but Budd paid them no mind. He swung his leg over his horse and situated himself in the saddle.

"Out of the way!" Evan shouted to the crowd outside the saloon.

Sadey led the group to the edge of town. They followed the main road until they reached mountainous terrain that cut through the landscape. The east road that Johnny spoke of was little more than a path... a path that Budd had chosen for the transports.

"This is all my fault," he grumbled bitterly. "I told the drivers to use the mountain paths into Sacramento to avoid the valley in case of ambushes. These narrow roads only allow for a single coach and a few guards, which would make it difficult for bandits to spot them at a distance."

"But it also leaves no chance of escape if the bandits do attack," Evan replied, somehow sensing where Budd's mind had wandered. "They'd be pinned down o—"

Sadey's gasp drew their attention to the road ahead. Hooves had battered the ground. Chunks of wood were strewn about, leading—like a trail of grim breadcrumbs—to the broken shrubs that lined the road. Beyond the shrubs was nothing but a steep cliff that hovered above the rapids.

"They went over..." Sadey's hushed tone caused Budd's head to spin.

He pulled his mare to a slow stop and jumped out of the saddle. Closer and closer, he crept toward the edge until the wreckage came into view. "They're alive!" he shouted with relief. But it was a fleeting relief, for Budd heard gunshots in the valley. His eyes flickered over the steep hills, dry underbrush, and patches of sand. "Over there! There's a path we can use to get to them on the other side."

"Going around would take too long," Evan argued.

Sadey grinned at them and replied, "We won't go around. We'll go across. I reckon we got three minutes of light on our side and we can use it to climb down. After that, it's just a matter of makin' it across the rapids."

Budd looked to the sliver of light just barely visible beyond the hills. They had no choice. "Evan, secure John to that tree over yonder. Sadey, grab the rest of the rope from my bag. We can wrap it around our waists." He braced his legs against two rocks to anchor his weight. "I'm the heaviest, so I'll go last. I can hold the two of you steady while you climb and then follow you down once you're near the bottom."

Evan scratched his head with a bewildered look in his eyes. "Are we really doing this? Seems like a one-way trip."

"We fall to our deaths, or we make it," Budd retorted. "Either way, going around ain't an option. There's barely any cover down there, and the men will run out of bullets if we don't hurry. We've got to try."

Chapter 12

East Road

Sacramento

Sweat dripped from Budd's furrowed brow. His fingers cramped as he held onto the rope. Evan and Sadey inched their way down the face of the cliff with careful steps. Budd's weight caused the stones he used to anchor himself to shift. Sadey's sudden screams were like a knife in the gut. Budd scrambled for the rope, catching it at the very end before it went over the edge. He looked down into the tear-streaked face of Sadey Conner.

"Talk to me! Anybody hurt?" he bellowed above the gunfire.

Sadey glanced down. "Evan fell!"

"Look at me," Budd urged. "Keep your eyes on me and keep climbing. Once you're at the bottom, try to help him."

When Sadey nodded her head, Budd tied the rope to one tree. Without Evan's weight, there was enough slack for Sadey to still get to the bottom. Budd returned to the cliff's edge and started his descent. He kept his hands firmly on the rope and walked down the wall of rock that still radiated heat from the sun.

"How are you doing, Sadey?"

'I made it,' she called up to him as she ducked behind the upturned stagecoach. "Evan broke his fall in the brush. He's unconscious, but he don't seem too hurt."

Budd muttered a quick prayer toward the darkened sky just as a hailstorm of bullets riddled the stones beside his feet. The outlaws had turned their attention to him. He took a deep breath for courage and let go of the rope. Shades of green and brown soared through his vision as he fell, hurtling toward the riverbank. Time stood still as Budd hit the water.

Waves crashed over his head. The force of the current pulled him under. Budd's fingers clawed at the bottom of the river, digging up stones and roots along the way. He pushed off a rock and gasped for air as his head bobbed just above the surface. Budd reached up to grasp a tree branch that dangled over the water and hauled himself out. Eyes burning, he scanned the riverbank for signs of the outlaws. The river had carried him about a quarter mile downstream, but he caught sight of four masked men hunkered down near an outcrop of stone.

The witnesses to the other attacks had said six men robbed the stagecoaches. Even if Budd added John Pepper, there was still one man unaccounted for—the leader. Whether that man was Ripley Eagleson or another outlaw, Budd had an awful feeling the leader of the gang would always be one step ahead of him. Things had gotten out of hand so quickly. Sacramento was supposed to have been Budd's fresh start, his chance at a normal life.

However, as he limped toward the gunfight up ahead, Budd realized he had ended up back where he started. The

Pinkertons were right about him. They said he was made for nothing more than hunting outlaws, that he would fight against them until he fought with them. Evan Farris and Sadey Conner had their reasons for breaking the law, but they were criminals.

And yet Budd still trusted Evan.

"Mansfield!" hollered a voice Budd recognized, snapping him out of his waterlogged train of thought. It was one of the stagecoach drivers. Budd hobbled over to the wrecked coach and squatted down. Pain throbbed in his ankle, but he pushed past it.

"What happened on the road?"

"It was all so fast," said the driver. "We were headed to town when the bandits showed up. They fired at us and then went for the strong box."

Budd took the rifle that was propped against a rock. "How many were hurt?"

"They shot two guards dead and then... I-I don't know. We went over the cliff after that." The driver's hand trembled and caused his pistol to shake. "Passengers are over by that big boulder."

Budd glanced over his shoulder and saw a sliver of a woman's shoe poking out from behind the huge hunk of stone. He thanked the good lord that most of the people had survived the attack, even if the fight wasn't quite over. "Follow the river until you reach a narrow path. We got one prisoner and some horses up there," Budd said. "Get those folks to town and have the sheriff send his deputies back to help us."

"I d-don't think I can."

Budd shook his head and grabbed the man by the front of his shirt. "Pull yourself together! There were a lot of things that I thought I couldn't do, but instead of whining about it, I did what I had to, to get through it."

The driver adjusted his hat and pulled out of Budd's hold. Budd watched as the man gathered his courage. He listened for a break in the gunfire and tapped the driver's shoulder. The driver raced over to the other side of the stagecoach, gathered the passengers, and started down the river's edge. It was a small victory that so many had survived.

"What happened?" Evan asked suddenly.

Out of the corner of his eye, Budd saw Evan stir. "About time you woke up," Budd snorted. "It's time to get to work."

***

Johnny tested the strength of his bonds with a few tugs. There was no give to the rope, and his hands had tingled from a lack of blood circulating through his arms. He looked around for anything sharp but came up short. Panic set in. Johnny rocked side to side. The bark of the tree rubbed his back raw, and the sound of cracking wood rang in his ears. Hope sprung anew. "Come on," he muttered. "Break, you overgrown twig!"

The tree groaned in protest, and Johnny sank his teeth into his bottom lip, giving one more hefty tug against the ropes. He tumbled to the side as the tree trunk snapped. Dry, rotted shards of wood stung the cuts that scored his back. Johnny hissed, rolling onto his knees and away from the termites that had made a home out of the old tree. He panted heavily as he struggled against a nauseating pain.

Voices came from somewhere down the road, and his icy panic returned. Johnny shook off the loose ropes before he crawled over to the horses. Budd Mansfield's mare gave him a scathing, side-eyed glance that Johnny felt down to his bones. He moved away from the barely tamed mount and pulled himself onto the back of a gangly stallion. The beast gave a wild buck, but Johnny yanked on the reins and forced it to submit.

The voices drew closer. Johnny steered the pilfered horse in the opposite direction. He moseyed along until he spotted the ambush trail. The gang must have followed the stagecoach down to the river somehow, he reckoned.

Each step along the steep, jagged passage caused the horse to pull against the reins in fear. Johnny kicked the beast in the side and jerked it back in the river's direction. "Move, you rotten horse!"

Gunshots got louder as they reverberated off the cliff wall. Johnny heard rushing water beneath the cacophony of bullets whizzing through the air. Black clouds of gunpowder puffed out of Leroy's old rifle each time he fired at the men behind the stagecoach. They had to think fast. Though the enemy's numbers were almost equal to the gang's. Johnny knew they wouldn't stand a chance without a diversion.

Budd Mansfield's speed was almost inhuman. He moved like a phantom, shrouded in shadow as he ducked behind his makeshift cover. Evan and that woman they baited Johnny with weren't too far behind. They moved like a well-oiled machine. When Mansfield whistled, the woman dashed over to his side and handed him some ammunition.

On the other side of the river, the gang bickered, shoved one another, and stole bullets out of each other's satchels. Their profanity and slurs were nearly as loud as the gunfight.

Rip would have noticed the gang's absence by now, but Johnny had learned long ago that his brother-in-law wasn't the sort of man to risk his operation for the lives of his men. Bandits and gunslingers were replaceable. Rip's carefully crafted image as an upstanding citizen, however, was something money couldn't buy. They were on their own. It was time Johnny stepped up.

Once the horse's hooves touched down on the riverbank, Johnny snapped the reins. He rode hard and fast to where the gang stood their ground. Hector immediately moved to help him out of the saddle, but Johnny slapped his hands away.

"Sorry I'm late to the party, fellas," he cackled. "Somebody hand me a dang gun before they kill us!"

Leroy unholstered his sidearm and passed it to Johnny. "Never thought I'd be happy to see you, Pepper."

Johnny ignored Leroy's retort and shifted his gaze over to Budd Mansfield. A look of pure hatred flashed in the man's eyes as he recognized Johnny. The outlaw couldn't help the way his lips pulled back into a toothy grin.

Evan Farris followed his partner's line of sight and realized Johnny had freed himself from the ropes. A sickeningly sweet wave of satisfaction washed over Johnny. He reveled knowing that Evan was no doubt reliving the torment of losing his family. Each time they locked eyes from across the river must have been like a slug to the chest. Their friendship had ended the day Johnny raided his hometown with his old gang. Evan had strayed down the path of an outlaw while Johnny had built himself a family.

"How did it feel, Farris?" Johnny heard himself asking. "How did it feel to meet Beatrice and our darling Kaitlyn?"

The shooting stopped suddenly.

Johnny straightened to his full height and slowly loaded rounds into his gun. "I bet you it felt like losing Dorothy and Joshua all over again," he continued. "I took your family away, and in return, I was blessed with a loving wife and a daughter who thinks I'm a hero. Funny how life is sometimes."

Evan stepped out from behind the stagecoach. Tears glistened in his eyes. He opened his mouth as if to speak, but it was too late. Johnny's distraction had worked to buy Hector some time. A spark flickered, and they launched a stick of dynamite at the stagecoach.

The gang dropped to the ground behind the rocks. An explosion sent shards of burning wood in every direction. Blackened debris littered the surrounding area.

Johnny coughed into his elbow, peering through the smoke and soot with squinted eyes. "Sound off," he croaked. "Leroy?"

"I'm all right."

"Hector?"

"Still alive, but it pinned Danny under this wheel," Hector replied. "We have to free his leg."

Johnny hurried over to Hector and Danny. He shoved his hand under the wheel and pushed up with all his might. The wheel creaked as it was raised off Danny's leg. Johnny let it fall once the youngest member of the gang was freed. They had shot Pete in the shoulder, Danny's leg was most likely broken, and Leroy had taken a nasty fall during the explosion.

"We're battered and bruised, but there's still some fight left in us," Johnny said. "Fall back before the smoke clears. We can patch ourselves up at the cache."

Chapter 13

Yosemite Valley

Cool water trickled over Budd Mansfield's hand. A high-pitched ring in his ears brought him back to reality. The last thing he remembered was a ball of fire coming right toward him. Budd had knocked Sadey to the ground before he lost consciousness, but the explosion must have catapulted them right into the water. Water that was considerably shallower than he last recalled.

Budd blinked past the burning in his eyes and looked up at the star-filled sky. If not for the aching pain in his body, he might have said it was a beautiful night. The scent of a forest and damp earth were as familiar to Budd as the back of his hand. He knew just by smell alone that he was no longer in the dry cliffs.

Instead, lush green trees greeted Budd as he finally sat upright. The river had taken him further east and down a waterfall. The gang was most likely miles away. John Pepper had stolen Evan's mount. With a bit of luck, Budd reckoned he'd be able to track the horse to wherever the bandits were holed up.

Evan's head emerged from the water with a great gasp. Budd shuffled over to his partner and offered his hand. "Help! I can't swim!"

"I got you," Budd said. "Deep breaths."

"Sadey! She—"

"I'll find her." Budd helped Evan up onto the smooth rocks that covered the riverbank. His partner coughed raggedly, but it wasn't long before his breathing returned to normal.

"Sadey went over first. I tried to grab onto her, but she dragged me under," Evan explained. "I had to let go…"

Budd nodded slowly as he calculated the odds that Sadey survived the fall. The waterfall towered over most of the valley. The jagged rocks surrounded the waterfall. Sadey could have hit many them on her way down.

Once Budd was sure Evan was all right, he scoured the riverbank for any sign of Sadey. The waterfall churned wildly and saturated the air with a dense mist. It blurred Budd's vision as he walked into the water until it reached his hips. Amid the foam and debris from the explosion, a head bobbed in and out of the water.

"Sadey, I'm coming!"

Dainty hands flailed desperately. She sputtered each time she surfaced. Feeble cries were drowned out by the unforgiving river. Budd swam as fast as he could, grabbing blindly into the water until he felt her arm. Sadey jumped into his arms. She clung to him like a startled cat, digging her nails into his shoulders.

Evan took Sadey from his arms when they reached the shore. Budd collapsed into the lush grass just beyond the river. The chill of the night air kept him awake, but he was exhausted.

"How did you make it down that waterfall without breaking every bone in your body?" Budd asked candidly. "Hell, I'm surprised I survived it."

Sadey shivered beside Evan. Her teeth clicked as she spoke. "I grabbed onto a piece of wood to stay afloat," she replied. "What was left of the stagecoach must have softened my landin'. My chest hurts and I can't feel my toes, but I'm alive."

Budd scrubbed his hand over his face. Frustration caused a muscle to tick in his jaw. "We need to start a fire, or else we ain't going to last an hour out here. Hopefully, the survivors got help in time."

Evan glanced up at the waterfall and said, "I could try to get back to the horses. Our supplies might still be there."

"We've got to be miles away," Budd argued, shaking his head. "It's pitch dark out. You've already fallen off a cliff and swept down a waterfall in the past few hours. I'm not about to let you go stumbling around in the forest at night."

Budd led out a groan as he stood up. Bears, cougars, and many wild animals lived in the valley. They needed a fire. He stepped lightly over the rocky riverbank until he reached the tree line. It hadn't rained in a few days, so Budd could collect some kindling for the fire. Evan built a circle of rocks and filled it with some larger pieces of wood.

"Come closer, Sadey," Budd ordered.

He struck two stones together as Evan puffed onto the sparks, breathing life into the fire. Sadey limped over to Budd's side and sat down to warm herself. Amber flames danced in her eyes. She lifted the bottom of her dress to her knees, revealing a long gash in her leg. Budd turned his back to Sadey to give her privacy. He punched Evan in the shoulder, urging his partner to do the same. Ruthless killer or not, Sadey was a lady.

"Y'all can turn around now," she said as she adjusted her clothing.

The sleeve of her dress was missing, so Budd assumed it had been used to wrap the wound. Her lack of fear impressed him. Most women would have been hysterical in their situation.

"What is that?" Evan asked suddenly.

Budd turned his gaze toward flickering lights in the trees. He reached for his gun before he realized it was gone. "Could be the sheriff," he told Evan. "Or prospectors."

The droll look on Evan's face nearly made Budd chuckle. Of course, there was a third possibility. After all, it could have been Johnny and the rest of the gang coming back to finish them off. They were waterlogged, cranky, and without weapons to defend themselves, but Budd wasn't ready to give up. It would take a lot more than John Pepper to break Budd Mansfield.

***

Sacramento

Steam wafted over the rim of Rip's cup. Burning hot coffee slid down his throat and eased the tension that had burrowed its way into his belly. A pocket watch sat before him, ticking as the seconds passed by. Each of those seconds added up into minutes and hours—hours without a single word from the gang. "I expected them back here by now,"

Rip told his sister. "They had explicit instructions. All those cowards had to do was run the wagon over the cliff, pop open the box, and send word once they were safe at the Old Mill."

Beatrice refilled Rip's cup with a brief hum of agreement. "Folks said they saw Budd Mansfield and that partner of his riding out of town. Sally told me they had a man tied up on the horse."

"Where to?"

"Somebody mentioned they might have headed east," she replied. "And that a woman had been riding with them."

Rip slammed his cup onto the table.

Beatrice gasped as she grabbed a rag from her apron. She dabbed away the scalding liquid from his skin. "Now don't you go burning yourself."

"I sent her to kill him! Budd Mansfield should be in an unmarked grave," Rip hollered. He stood up and launched his fist at the wall. Plaster crumbled beneath the force of his rage. White dust fell to the floor and covered his coffee-stained sleeve. "If that husband of yours had anything to do with this—"

"Uncle Rip?"

All the anger left Rip's body when Kaitlyn's sweet voice reached his ears. He dusted off the plaster from his knuckles and lifted the small child into his arms. She blinked her sleepy eyes up at him, stealing his black heart away with each flutter of her lashes.

"Sorry I woke you, darling," he whispered. "Come on. Let's get you back to bed." Rip nodded to his sister and headed for the staircase.

Beatrice smiled his way as she cleaned up the spill, not at all bothered by his sudden shift in mood. He reckoned it happened often enough that she had grown accustomed to his fits. But nothing could change his scowl into a smile quicker than the little angel in his arms. Kaitlyn was his world.

"Everything I do is for you. You know that, right?" he whispered, and Kaitlyn nodded her little head. "No matter what anyone might say, I did it so you could live a good life. You don't have to be like me or your papa, Kitty."

She reached her arms up and pressed her hand flat against his smooth cheek. Even at her young age, Kaitlyn had seen far more than any child should have . It was easy to put the blame on John, but Rip knew he was part of the problem. Kaitlyn deserved better than a family of swindlers and outlaws. She deserved all the crowns and castles that she dreamed about each night.

Rip carried her to bed, tucked her under the covers, and kissed her forehead. He waited until those sleepy eyes closed before he shuffled back downstairs, where Beatrice pounded a lump of dough with a rolling pin.

"You should leave that for the servants," Rip suggested as he fished a cigar from his pocket. "That's why I pay them to be here."

"The maids are too busy washing blood from the clothes in the scullery to be bothered with the baking." There was scorn in her tone that betrayed the smile on her face. "Things might be different if this was a working ranch."

"You got horses and livestock—not to mention plenty of farmhands and maids to handle the rest. There's money in the safe and food in your belly. What more do you want from me?"

Beatrice glared up from her worktable and replied, "Every morning I write letters to your men pretending to be their wives. I tell them their families are living well off the money from the robberies."

"I wouldn't ask it of you if I thought for one second you couldn't handle it." Rip sighed, smoke leaking from his nostrils. "It'll get better."

"The guilt I feel each time I smile and hand them a plate to eat… it's tearing me apart." Beatrice set down the rolling pin and dusted her hands off onto her apron. "After all the lies and the tears, I drive the wagon into town and hear the whispers—whispers that my husband is a thief and a killer."

"He is."

"But you promised me no one would suspect a thing. That Johnny would be safe." She sniffled. "I don't want to be like everyone else in this godforsaken town. I don't want to be just another person you lie to."

Rip pulled the cigar from between his teeth and walked over to his sister. He blew a cloud of smoke into her face as he spoke. "Careful, Beatrice," Rip growled. "Don't blame me for John's foolishness. I gave you this life of luxury, and I can take it away in the blink of an eye. I have never and will never lie to you."

"All that we are and all we have is tainted by the innocent blood you and John spill." Beatrice's lip wobbled as she asked, "How can you expect me to live with that? How am I supposed to live with these lies?"

"I suggest you find a way," Rip answered with a shrug. He tapped his cigar on the edge of the table. Ashes fell onto the small pile of plaster. "Because if you don't, I'll take Kaitlyn."

"Y-you can't do that."

"I can and I will. I will take her far from here, and you will never see her again." He moved toward the back door with quick, easy steps. "I'll give her a new family, one that will not hesitate to soil their palms so she may have the life you and I have never had."

Chapter 14

Bandit Cache

Yosemite Valley

"Get inside!" Johnny shouted. Danny's unconscious body was draped over his shoulders.

The young man had just collapsed after having walked six or seven miles from where he was injured. They had sent Pete and Hector to ready the cabin, and Leroy cared little about anyone but himself, so that left Johnny to carry the burden. He hadn't minded so much. Danny was a decent enough fellow that Johnny almost felt bad for the way they tangled him up with Rip.

Hector threw open the door before Leroy even grasped the handle. One look at Danny's leg made the man's face pale. Johnny shoved past the lot of them and dumped Danny onto a cot in the corner. He grabbed a half-empty, warm beer bottle from the table near the barren hearth. The first sip wasn't so bad, but the more he drank, the more his stomach turned.

"We need to talk," Hector said.

Johnny avoided Hector's prying gaze. "Talk about what, exactly?" He flopped down onto a chair near the cot.

"Danny," Hector answered. "I have seen what can happen to a crushed leg without a doctor tending it. The skin goes black and sickness takes hold."

"Danny will be fine," Leroy interjected from beside the door. The rifle in his clutches was old and rusted at the end of the barrel.

The interruption only deterred Hector for a second. He continued, "And I would also like to know why you showed up at the same time as those gringos."

Johnny finally met Hector's stare. He set the beer aside and propped his feet up on the table. "I don't think I like what you're insinuating."

Hector knocked Johnny's feet down with a scowl. The large man crossed his arms over his chest, seemingly unfazed by the change in Johnny's tone. "Rip will want an answer. You are lucky that I am asking, and not him."

"Rip," Johnny scoffed irritably. Of course, the gang wanted nothing more than to run back to their leader like a bunch of children. "Who cares about Rip? My brother-in-law ain't got to ask anything because I didn't tell those fools what they wanted to hear!"

"But you led them to us."

"Because I knew we could handle them," Johnny explained. "Mansfield don't know nothing, Hector. It ain't like he's a lawman or anything. Despite what Rip wants you to think, Mansfield is not our problem."

"I have fought Mansfield," Hector argued. "He's more of a problem than the sheriff and the deputies. They never would have been able to trap one of us—"

A loud crash came from the kitchen.

Johnny scowled as he stood up and stomped out of the room. He found Pete banging around in the cupboards, tossing cans and empty cigarette packets over his shoulder.

He had his hand clutched over a gunshot wound. There was a pale cast on the outlaw's face.

Sweat beaded on Pete's upper lip as he collapsed against the table. "I need bandages, man!" Pete shouted desperately. "This thing is goin' to get infected."

"It'd be much less than you deserve," Johnny retorted. "Sit down."

He shoved Pete into the chair and snatched Hector's satchel. He dumped three rolls of bandages and some pills onto the table. Hector stormed out of the kitchen just as a blood-chilling scream erupted from the bedroom. Johnny shook his head to rid himself of any thoughts other than getting the gang out alive.

Rip hadn't come for them yet, so Johnny figured they were on their own. Hell, his brother-in-law most likely knew they were in trouble and helped himself to another glass of brandy rather than risk his hide for them. On any other occasion, Johnny wouldn't have bothered patching up Pete's wound or caring about Danny's leg. But he needed them to get him as far away from Sacramento as possible.

"We got to run," he mumbled.

Pete's brow furrowed as he leaned closer. "You're a dang madman if you think—"

"Mansfield ain't like the sheriff. He'll come for us the second he's able." Johnny handed the unknown pills to Pete and continued, "We can take the money and lie low in Nevada. I got a cousin up there who'll take us in for a while."

"Ain't no way I'm gonna leave Rip high and dry like some yellow-bellied ingrate."

"You might not have a choice," Johnny snapped. "Hector and Leroy know you and Danny will slow us down if we trek back to Sacramento. They'll leave you behind without a second thought. I don't want to see that happen." It wasn't often Johnny preyed upon the last bit of humanity within the outlaws of the gang, but he wasn't willing to face the hangman's noose anytime soon.

"Say we get away with the money," Pete began. "What happens then? What's goin' to keep you from puttin' a bullet in my head the second we reach the border?"

Johnny sensed more than accusations in Pete's voice. He sensed anger. "Let me guess. You heard about what I did to Cornwall?" he asked, and Pete nodded his head in reply. "Well, I only killed him because Rip made me do it. You heard him barking at me plenty of times. I had no choice… it was Cornwall or me, and I chose to live."

"Killin' ain't Rip's way unless he has no other option."

Johnny slammed his palm on the table, causing Pete to jump. "He might not be the one pulling the trigger anymore, but he's a killer. A killer who will do whatever it takes to make sure his perfect life ain't tampered with."

Understanding seemed to have finally reached Pete's dense mind. "And keepin' us around would be bad news for him, seein' as the law is on our tail now. He's goin' to let us take the fall for everythin'."

The door to the kitchen opened. Suspicion flashed in Leroy's dark blue gaze as he wiped his hands on a rag. "Danny's alive, but he lost the leg. We'll know if it's infected tomorrow if he wakes up with a fever."

***

Yosemite Valley

For the first time since he traveled to the west, Budd was delighted to see the rising sun. He even welcomed the sweltering heat after the cold air that had cradled them most of the night. If not for Sheriff Dawson and his deputies arriving when they had, Budd suspected he might not have lived long enough to see the dawn. But the warm clothes, dry bedroll, and oatmeal the sheriff provided were as close to home as he had been in a long time. "Thank you," Budd said. "For everything."

"From what Lincoln told me, none of the passengers would have made it out of the cliffs without you and Evan Farris. It would be a betrayal on my part if I had let you die out here. We had to come find you."

Budd clapped Sheriff Dawson on the shoulder in thanks. "I'm grateful."

"We'll head back to the crash to retrieve what we can, but that explosion might have done away with anything useful to our case," grumbled the sheriff. "Looks like all we got is the witness statements to warrant John Pepper's arrest. Even then, it ain't enough to see him brought to justice."

"It's about a day's ride back to Sacramento." Budd scratched at the shadow of a beard on his chin. "The gang could be across the border by then, and we can't let that happen."

"What do you have in mind?"

"Take Sadey back with you," he replied. "She's hurt, and we can't have her getting an infection or slowing us down."

"You're going after them? Alone?" Sheriff Dawson suddenly glanced over at Evan. There was a guarded look on his face as he asked, "Are you ready to ride to your death with him?"

"Evan and I have to see this through," Budd answered. "Sadey will lead you to our horses. If we don't make it back by nightfall, then send help."

Sheriff Dawson looked ready to argue, but he held his tongue. The lawman had his way of doing things, and Budd understood—even admired—his dedication to the job. However, John Pepper wasn't the sort of man who respected the authority that came with a badge.

"I'll agree to this under one condition," Sheriff Dawson said as he handed Budd and Evan a pair of single-action revolvers. He hesitated once more before retrieving two badges from his saddlebag. "You go after Pepper, and you do it right. The badges are temporary, but make sure you uphold the law when you wear them—that means keeping John Pepper alive so he can go to trial. It ain't our place to decide the fate of others. That's between a judge and the good Lord above."

Budd shook the sheriff's hand. He pinned the badge to his borrowed vest and shoved the fancy new firearm into his holster. The clean shine on the weapon was just one more reminder that the world had changed. "Thank you kindly, Sheriff."

"I can't believe you think that I—" Evan drew up short. He winced as he looked down at the badge in his hand. "John Pepper… All right, yeah, w-we'll bring him back alive."

Budd watched his partner closely. He supposed accepting the badge had meant a lot more to Evan than most people, for the man had earned the sheriff's trust at the cost of avenging his family.

"What about the rest of the gang?" Budd asked. "Are we bringing them in alive too? They outnumber my partner and I as it is."

Sheriff Dawson shut his eyes for a moment. He smoothed his finger over the furrow in his brow as he considered Budd's questions. "John is our priority… even if that means letting the others go for now. He's the only one we can place at the robberies and the driver's murder. If we're going to get him for everything else, we have to question him. Maybe he'll give us names or a way into their hideout."

"Understood." Budd nodded his head as he kicked dirt onto the remnants of their campfire. He watched as Sheriff Dawson and his deputies saddled up for their ride back to town. Sadey glanced over her shoulder at Budd. There was something dark and conflicting in her gaze that he couldn't quite read. He had only known Sadey for a short while, but it had been long enough that Budd saw just how vulnerable she was behind her deadly reputation.

Sadey could have double-crossed them at any time. Lord knew Budd and Evan had been so caught up in finding the gang that she had plenty of opportunity. That she hadn't attempted to kill him again had restored a bit of Budd's faith in the world. The idea gave him a spark of hope that perhaps he had changed more than he realized.

"You ready?" Evan asked. "It's a long walk ahead of us. We should get going before the gang moves on."

Budd adjusted the strap of his satchel and started off down the rocky shore of the riverbank. "Maybe we can cut across those peaks over there to make up for lost time."

"I hope that ain't your idea of a joke. I nearly died the last time you made me climb."

"Don't you whine now," Budd snorted.

Evan followed behind Budd, grumbling under his breath along the way. Brilliant streaks of gold and sapphire stretched across the horizon. Birds chirped in the treetops, breaking up the sounds of the rushing rapids as the fog lifted.

Hours passed. Budd and Evan trekked across the landscape until they reached the blackened stone and charred wood left behind by the explosion. The smell of sulfur and char clung to the morning breeze.

Chapter 15

Bandit Cache

Yosemite Valley

The door opened. It hit the wall with a deafening thud.

Pete gasped and panted like he had run the entire distance of the valley—and he just might have. He held his bandaged arm with a clammy hand as he met Johnny's stare. "Mansfield… he's alive," Pete said. "And he's tracked us here from the river."

"How much time do we have?" Johnny grabbed the bag beside the bedroom door and opened the clasps. Two rifles and a handful of pistols were haphazardly strewn atop stacks of cash, bonds, and precious jewels pilfered from the stagecoach. Johnny loaded one of the old rifles and hurried over to the window.

A shadow moved among the trees. Johnny cursed quietly. The gang had run out of time. Mansfield and his partner stood just at the edge of Johnny's line of sight. They were close enough that he hadn't mistaken their identities, but far enough that he couldn't get a bead on them. His rifle swayed as he watched Mansfield. The sheer audacity and fearlessness the man exuded were almost enough to make Johnny run for it.

But he held his position and cocked the rifle. The sound carried, alerting Mansfield that his approach was unwelcome.

"Stay right there," Johnny called. He lifted his hand, and the others tugged black scarves and bandanas over their faces. They loaded rounds into their weapons, eyes locked on Mansfield as Johnny smiled tauntingly. "I saw you floating in the river and thought luck was finally on my side."

"I'm afraid not," Mansfield said. "Might want to abandon hope, too, while you're at it. Because I'm not giving up until one of us is dead or clapped in irons."

Though Mansfield had donned fresh clothes and stood with a confidence most outlaws failed to replicate, Johnny saw the dark circles under those stony eyes. He saw the rough stubble on his jaw and the unruly locks upon his head. Mansfield was at the end of his rope. A man with a shiny new deputy's badge pinned to his chest. Johnny wondered to himself if that might help him.

Pete winced as he moved to Johnny's side with the second rifle. "Hector and Leroy are gone. They took off out the back door with the money."

Dang. Johnny wasn't sure if he was hurt by their actions or impressed they had pulled off exactly what he had planned to do to them. He sucked his teeth with a shake of his head. "Danny's no use to us with one leg. There's still time to—"

A bullet grazed Johnny's cheek. Red-hot pain scorched his flesh as he bit back a scream. He saw a blur of motion out of the corner of his eye. Mansfield had tackled his partner to the ground. They wrestled over the gun, momentarily distracted. Johnny took aim with his rifle once more and fired at the two men. Mansfield shoved his partner behind the trees. Bullets kicked up dirt as they hit the ground. Shells pinged off the floor beside Johnny's boots before they rolled out of sight.

Gunpowder burned Johnny's eyes, and thick plumes of black soot showed the old rifle was struggling to keep up with the rate as he squeezed the trigger. "Run while you still can, Mansfield! And put down that tired old dog you got following you around. Farris ain't nothing more than the shadow of a man."

Evan Farris leaped out from behind the tree and darted for the cabin. He swerved and dodged bullets. Glass shattered as he came crashing through the window, knocking Johnny to the floor. The rifle bucked and blasted a hole in the ceiling as Evan tried to wrestle it from his hands. Once more, Johnny found himself at his old friend's mercy. Evan's sweaty fingers wrapped around his neck, squeezing until spots danced in his vision.

"Evan!" Mansfield barked. "We need him alive."

Pratt Dempcy & Company was smart to have hired Mansfield, Johnny thought to himself as Evan's hold loosened up a bit. The man was built like a brick wall. Wide shoulders cast an imposing shadow upon Johnny where he lay on the floor. But Mansfield's eyes widened at the kiss of steel against the nape of his neck. Johnny balled his hand into a fist and jabbed Evan in the ribs.

"Lower your weapon," Pete stammered to Mansfield as he watched Evan curl up on his side. "What's the point in comin' all this way for it to end like this?"

Johnny stood up and kicked Evan. "Shoot him," he ordered Pete. Even with Pete's mask in place, it wasn't hard for Johnny to note the disapproval in the outlaw's eyes. Rip's speeches kept the men loyal, even when faced with imminent danger. It was a mentality Johnny hadn't quite grasped. "Ain't no way we get free if we keep them alive."

Pete remained silent.

A pained groan came from the bedroom. Mansfield spun his gun and aimed right at Johnny. "Who's in there?"

"The rest of the gang," Johnny snorted. "Did you think we'd go back to Sacramento without a fight?"

Evan made a grab for the gun on the floor. Johnny stomped on Evan's fingers before he kicked the gun away. Mansfield unholstered his backup sidearm. Pete shot first, but Evan kicked the outlaw's legs, causing his arm to jerk at the last second. Plaster fell from the wall. Mansfield fired and his aim was true.

Pete stumbled back.

The bullet hit him in the leg opposite his wounded arm. Johnny capitalized on the distraction and tackled Mansfield. They hit the wall. A picture fell from the mantle of the fireplace, frame splintering upon impact. Kaitlyn and Beatrice's faces peered up at Johnny from the image as he grappled with Mansfield. Out of the corner of his eye, he glimpsed Pete as the coward escaped out the back door.

"Go after him!" Mansfield shouted to Evan. Rapid footfalls echoed in the cabin, followed by the unmistakable sound of horses outside.

Anger overwhelmed Johnny, and he bashed the end of the pistol against Mansfield's head. Over and over, he hit

Mansfield. Johnny struggled with the weapon even when the newly deputized man had blacked out from multiple blows to the skull. Budd Mansfield fought as best he could while he came in and out of consciousness.

Some part of John recognized it as an animal instinct to fight. He even respected it a little.

Johnny growled, released Mansfield long enough to grab Pete's discarded rifle, and pulled the trigger. A puff of black powder sputtered from the muzzle, blinding Johnny to his surroundings. As the weapon misfired, Mansfield squeezed off four rounds. The first missed, getting lodged in the wall behind them. But the last three bullets, with the accuracy of a sharpshooter, hit Johnny in the center of his chest.

***

Sacramento
Five days later...

"Hey, partner," a voice said from somewhere in the darkness of Budd's mind. He clawed his way through the fog, inching closer and closer to the surface of his consciousness. Light broke through the shadows as he peeled his eyes open. Evan stood over Budd, prodding along the edge of the bandage on Budd's head. "You gave us all quite a scare. I won't lie. Thought you'd never wake up."

"John," Budd croaked. His throat burned something fierce. "Is he...?"

"Yeah, he's dead. We arrested the man they had hidden in the bedroom, but the rest of the gang is in the wind." Evan pulled back his hand and rubbed his tired eyes. "Sheriff

Dawson showed up not long after you passed out. His deputies went after the outlaws."

"What did they find?"

"We don't know," Evan said grimly. "It's been three days, and they haven't sent a word. Sheriff is waiting a little while longer before he declares them missing."

Budd tried to sit up, but Evan laid a firm hand on his chest, pushing him back onto the mattress. He took in his surroundings and found himself in the town's infirmary. Nurses shuffled quietly through the room, tending to other patients. "How long have I been here?"

"Five days." Evan ran fingers through his hair. "Sheriff Dawson knows what happened. He knows it was you or Johnny walking away from that brawl. Johnny just…. He ain't give you much of a choice. I still haven't told his family."

"I'll do it," Budd replied. "It should come from me."

He stood up slowly, brushing Evan's hands away when he attempted to push him back onto the bed. Budd stretched high above his head until his spine cracked. The blow to his head had knocked him unconscious for nearly a week, but Budd knew his job wasn't done. Far from it.

"A letter for you, Mr. Mansfield," said a nurse as she smiled up at him kindly. She dug around in her apron and brought out a yellowed envelope.

Budd recognized the writing beneath the spatter of stamps. He ripped open the envelope without hesitation. "Rose was worried when I didn't write. She purchased a train ticket and intends to arrive by Christmas."

"That… that ain't good, my friend."

Evan had said what Budd already knew. The roads weren't safe. Passage through California was limited—even without the bandits attacking stagecoaches. Outlaws and hired guns from Mexico were everywhere, robbing trains as far as Texas and lying low in cities like Sacramento.

Though the law had fought to establish peace, the west was no place for a lady like Rose Buchanan. No, she was better off being pampered by her well-off family than risking her life on the road for the likes of Budd Mansfield.

"I'll write to her and tell her not to come."

"Is that for her sake or Sadey's?" Evan asked boldly.

Budd wasn't sure. "Sadey knows where my heart lies."

"Doesn't mean it won't hurt her to meet Rose."

"That's why I need to keep my promise and get her out of Sacramento before Rip Eagleson or Rose ever cross her path," he said. "Whatever affection she had for me will be long gone when she starts her new life."

Evan shook his head and gave Budd a moment alone. Budd changed into the clothes Evan found for him, shaved with the blade provided by the nurse, and shook hands with the doctor before leaving the infirmary. He stepped into the morning air and felt the sun on his face. "I thought I would not make it out of that valley. But God was on my side."

"Let's hope he sticks around to see this thing through," Evan snorted.

Budd brushed a hand over the front of his vest and began his stroll toward the hotel beside the post office. He kept his eyes trained on the only room with the curtains pulled closed on such a beautiful morning. The owner greeted Budd and Evan the second they walked through the door. They tipped their hats, sauntering up the stairs with a confident swagger.

An ache unfurled at Budd's temple, but he ignored it. He lifted his hand and knocked four times on the door of room 203. A cacophony of bangs and clangs seeped through the cracks in the door. Budd smiled slightly and bolted for the back door. He looked up just as Sadey Conner's leg appeared through an open window. She shimmied down the side of the hotel, hitting the ground beside an overflowing bag. Sleeves of partially concealed dresses flapped in the wind as she picked up her luggage—still unaware Budd had witnessed her escape.

"Going somewhere?"

Sadey let out a squeal as she whirled around toward the sound of Budd's voice. "I could've shot you!" she hissed. "What the blazes are you doin' here, Mansfield? I thought you were a goner."

"Not quite." Budd helped Sadey with her bag just as Evan rounded the corner. His partner collapsed against the wall in a fit of laughter at Sadey's expense. She made quite the sight with her skirts rumpled and her hair strewn about in a mane of unruly waves. It was clear her hasty attempt at an escape hadn't been planned.

"Hush up," Sadey said, even as a smile tugged at the corners of her rosy lips. "I thought you were… someone else. Anyway, I need to get out of this city. I stuck around to make sure Budd hadn't kicked it, but now I have to leave before Rip finds me."

"Head down to see Sheriff Dawson," Evan replied. "He and I came to an agreement that you deserve a reward for helping us take down the bandits who robbed the stagecoach."

Budd remained quiet, unaware they had met such an agreement.

Evan continued, "He has two deputies waiting to escort you out of Sacramento. They'll take you all the way to Nevada, where a marshal is waiting to escort a caravan further east."

"I-I don't understand."

"I think what my partner is saying," Budd interjected. "Is that we're keeping our promise to get you out of the west. With the reward money, you'll be able to start a new life."

Sadey, the hardened killer for hire, threw herself at Budd and wrapped her arms around his middle. Tears soaked into his vest as ragged hiccups met his ears. She lifted her head. Eyes like big sparkling jewels stared up at him. "I didn't think you would keep your word," Sadey whispered. "I thought you would leave me to face the gruesome end I deserve."

Budd untangled himself from her arms, blushing from the tips of his ears to the bottoms of his feet. He took a step back and cleared his throat. "I, uh, always keep my word."

Chapter 16

The Old Mill
Yosemite Valley

Storm's hooves battered the dirt along the trail. The large stallion snorted and tossed his mane, vicious and wild as his rider. Ripley Eagleson leaned over the horse, blinking away the bits of dust that floated up into his eyes. His expression was blank despite the hatred he felt inside. It was like the lid on a pot struggling to keep a stew from bubbling over.

Behind him rode two masked men. Their pale white horses tore through the underbrush alongside his dark mount until the Old Mill was in sight. Rip slowed to a stop and whistled sharply. A shadow appeared in a large, greasy window high above his head. "Let us in right now!"

The gate opened slowly as Rip glared up at the figure in the window until it trembled. He signaled for the others to ride ahead and then led Storm into the courtyard. If not for an overzealous businessman trying to get ahead of the modern world, their fortress wouldn't have existed. After all, with talks of railroad expansion, someone had to forge the components to aid development. But the building had never been finished. Its construction was frozen in time for the past two years.

The empty munition crates, clunky helmets, and rusted scraps of metal in the courtyard usually brought a smile to his face. They served as a reminder to anyone who wanted to take the old steel mill for themselves that even the army hadn't been able to defeat the outlaws who had laid claim to it. Four gangs of outlaws had come and gone, leaving behind their mark.

Rip had worked his way up in the ranks of the Desert Raiders. He had built a reputation not unlike the one Johnny had. And when their leader let down his guard, Rip had been the one to serve the man's head to his own men on a silver platter. The gang disbanded, and those loyal to Rip had stuck by his side—at least until Budd Mansfield arrived in Sacramento.

"Leroy!"

"Rip, I told them not to—"

A thunderous slap across his face cut Leroy's words off. Rip grabbed the man by the back of his neck and yanked him close. "Tend to the horses," he whispered harshly. "And then meet us inside."

"Yes, boss." Leroy scurried over to Storm and the other mounts as Hector opened the doors. Rip removed his hat and walked over the threshold. A cavernous room greeted him on the other side. A table sat at the center, six cots lined the far right wall, and three safes were all that filled the space. Hector and Leroy were all that remained of the gang he sent into the valley. But Rip had a solution for his lack of outlaws. Well, two solutions.

The men who had ridden to the Old Mill with Rip removed their masks.

Hector sucked in a sharp breath and took a step away from them. "Boss, we should talk about what happened with Johnny... before you decide."

"Salazar and Charles are here by my request, Hector," Rip replied. "Their time in prison came to an abrupt end once they received my letter, and it would be a dishonor if I turned my back on their show of unity. After all, I find myself short of a few men."

"Danny lost his leg. We couldn't bring him along."

"I know what happened!" he snapped. "Danny... succumbed to his injuries, but Johnny and Pete were supposed to make it back here with you. Am I just supposed to forgive you for leaving my darling sister's husband to die at the hands of Budd Mansfield?"

"No, sir."

Rip pulled out a chair and took a seat. He nodded toward Leroy as he walked through the door after tending to the horses. "You two have to earn my forgiveness. Starting now. And you can start by informing our friends, Salazar and Charles, about our plans for Pratt Dempcy & Company."

****

Sacramento

Budd pushed through the door of the sheriff's office that afternoon. Three deputies blocked his view of a cell. Sheriff Dawson noticed Budd and gestured for him to move closer. In the cell was a man hunkered over a beaten up cot. His head hung as he wept. Budd could not identify the outlaw who Sheriff Dawson's men captured in the valley, but the eagle tattoo on his forearm marked him as a member of the gang responsible for the stagecoach robberies.

"I left him," muttered the man. "I left Johnny to die and now… now the boss is goin' to kill me dead!" Whatever cold-blooded cruelty had allowed the outlaw to rob and murder was gone. Left in its place was a slobbering coward.

"We thought you might want to ask him some questions," said Sheriff Dawson. "I got all I needed out of him. Whatever else he knows won't help us, but it might help your case."

Budd patted the sheriff on the shoulder and let himself into the cell. "You were found not too far from a known bandit outpost in Yosemite Valley," Budd began. "And you had a stack of cards in your pocket, only consisting of aces of spades. It's something we've been associating with a gang of outlaws targeting Pratt Dempcy & Company stagecoaches."

"I-I don't know nothin'."

"Really?" he asked. "Funny. My friend Sheriff Dawson said you were quite talkative when he questioned you. Cat got your tongue suddenly?"

The man turned his head toward Budd and flinched. "Nah, sir. Just… I was told men like me don't make it to a trial once they've talked to Budd Mansfield."

A pang of regret started in the pit of Budd's stomach and slithered up to his throat. It tasted of bitterness and bile. "I'm not in the business of hunting outlaws anymore."

"That ain't what it looks like from here."

"What's your name?" Budd asked. "You know mine."

"Pete."

"Well, Pete, the bandage on your leg and the tattoo on your arm identify you as the man who nearly shot my partner." Budd stepped toward Pete as he hooked his thumbs in the belt loops of his trousers. "Whether or not you had the ace of spades, we got enough to send you away for a long time. You shot at deputies, evaded lawmen, and fled from the scene of a stagecoach robbery."

"Send me away! It's better than facing… him."

"Who's got you so scared, Pete?" Budd inquired. "Is it Ripley Eagleson?" He moved ever closer until he came face to face with the prisoner. Budd placed a hand on Pete's shoulder and continued, "Don't protect him. Ripley Eagleson's place in the civilized world is getting smaller and smaller."

"No! That… I didn't say that! You said it, not me!" Pete knocked Budd's hand away and tripped over the cot. He curled up, cradling his injured leg.

"You would rather rot in a cell or be hanged than admit he's the puppet master? That he's the one pulling the strings behind all this?" Budd's voice boomed in the small cell. He felt Sheriff Dawson tug him back, but Budd shrugged him off. "What does he have over you? Huh?"

"My family needs money. That's why I robbed the stagecoaches. Just me and Johnny. Nobody else." A blank expression appeared on Pete's face. "Nobody."

"Six riders. That's how many men the witness, Mr. Cornwall, saw the day the stagecoach driver was murdered. And the passengers you ran off the road saw five. I'm not a mathematician, Pete, but that don't add up to me."

"Just me and Johnny."

Budd knew he had hit another wall in his investigation. Pete wasn't willing to turn on Eagleson, so Budd had to find someone who would. He stepped out of the cell and closed it behind him. Sheriff Dawson looked slightly peeved, but Budd wasn't concerned. Deadly outlaws had escaped. It was a mistake that needed rectifying.

Evan waited outside with the horses. They rode to Haven Ranch with the expectation of finding a distressed widow and child. However, what greeted them was anything but that. Loud music streamed through open windows as curtains fluttered in the breeze. Voices carried on the wind that were jovial instead of mournful. He would have wagered half the folks in Timber were inside the ranch house. Budd kept his expression in check as he knocked upon the door.

A man with a thick beard and bushy eyebrows answered. "What do you want?"

"Sir, may I speak to Mrs. Beatrice Pepper?" Budd asked.

"She ain't here."

"Excuse me? This is her family's ranch."

"Not anymore," said the strange man. "This here ranch belongs to the Calloways now, mister. My pa bought it from the Peppers on account of John dying and all. Got it for a good price too. I saw Beatrice and her daughter heading out of town."

The door shut in Budd's face.

He stood upon the front porch, unable to fully comprehend what Mr. Calloway had revealed. Ripley Eagleson continued to strut about the city unharmed and untouched by the unusual changes that had taken place in the wake of Budd's investigation. It seemed everyone except the man Budd suspected of treachery paid the price for the crimes against Pratt Dempcy & Company.

"Johnny is dead, and his partner is behind bars," Evan called from the top of his horse. "We did what we could with the information we had to go on. Don't beat yourself up over all this. Consider what we've accomplished as a victory. The bandits will think twice before they hit another stagecoach."

Budd pulled himself up into the saddle, still dizzy from his time on bedrest. He pinched the bridge of his nose and sighed. "The world is a better place without John Pepper in it. But I won't stop until all of them are brought to justice."

Epilogue

Sacramento

Budd watched the clock on the wall with tired eyes. The solicitor sat at his desk across from Budd and Evan, quietly scratching away at a notepad with his pencil. Mr. Jordan Jeffers saw to all legal and ethical matters associated with Pratt Dempcy & Company, so Budd had met with the twitchy little man in the past. Evan Farris, however, didn't have the pleasure until the death of John Pepper.

"Let us go over the events that transpired on November the fifteenth again, shall we?" Mr. Jeffers huffed.

"It was morning when Evan and I found the cabin," Budd answered with a low rumble in his voice. Three times they had been over what happened. "We had spent the entire night following the trail left behind by the outlaws. I wanted to approach cautiously, so I tried talking John down."

"And then Mr. Pepper fired his weapon at you and your partner?"

"Heated words were exchanged and then… yeah, they shot at us from the window." Budd's answer was followed by yet another detailed description of the fight that had cost a man his life. When the story came to the same conclusion as before, Budd looked to Mr. Thayer.

"You did well, son," Mr. Thayer said finally. "In fact, Mr. Jeffers is here to make your promotion to manager of security more official."

"What about Evan?"

"He may keep his rank as deputy if Sheriff Dawson permits it and work with you on your continuing efforts to find these bandits." Mr. Thayer and the solicitor packed up their briefcases. "You know where to find us if you should require my assistance."

Budd and Evan shook hands with Mr. Thayer and Mr. Jeffers. It was nearly two o'clock when Budd and Evan left the solicitor's office and made their way down to the saloon for a drink. Budd ordered a beer, and Evan had a glass of whiskey. The alcohol helped ease the tangle of nerves in Budd's belly.

"Another day of this mess and I'll happily step in front of a moving wagon," he joked. "Bureaucracy is a pain in my rear."

Evan snorted and coughed, choking slightly on his whiskey. "I'm not big on politics myself, but I understand Thayer wanting to be careful. It's solicitors I don't like."

"Seems like you'll have to get used to it if you plan on wearing that badge any longer."

Evan removed his hat and settled into his seat. "I'll give it some thought. Never imagined myself as a man of the law." He pulled three letters out of his pocket and slid them across the table. "These came for you this morning. Lost in the post."

"Rose?"

Evan nodded.

Budd tore open the most recent letter and cringed. "She'll arrive tomorrow."

"What? I thought you—"

"I wrote to her and said not to make the trip, but it seems too late," Budd muttered. "She left Boston in September, and she was in Reno when she sent this."

"How did you two meet, anyway? I don't think you've ever said."

"She was one of my only friends when I was a boy," Budd revealed. "It was Rose, me, and Douglas raising hell together until she moved away with her mother. A daughter of old money. The kind that made folks like you and me seem like beggars in comparison."

"She married?"

Budd nodded, but said nothing further. Instead, he drank until the night faded away and gave birth to the dawn. Shadows still covered most of the city when he and Evan walked down to the stables. People arrived in wagons packed to the brim with bags of goods to sell to the merchants, and the stagecoach appeared on the horizon just as the sun peeked behind the hills.

Budd's heart leaped in his chest even as he was struck by the sudden urge to run for cover. Love did crazy things to him he struggled to understand. Just the thought of Rose traveling so far from home to see him was... Well, it was enough to drive him mad with worry. "Lord, give me strength."

After three train rides, two wagon rides, and a stagecoach, Rose stepped onto the sidewalk. Budd wasn't ready. His hands turned clammy, and the heat of his blush threatened to scorch the earth until it was nothing but ashes. He rocked on his heels the moment he laid his gaze upon her golden locks. A smile blossomed on her lips when she caught sight of him staring. He was a fool in love, and Budd reckoned she was all too aware of that fact.

"Mr. Mansfield," Rose whispered.

"Miss—er—Mrs. Buchanan." Budd tipped his hat to her and moved to shake hands with Rose's husband, Douglas. "I hope your travels were pleasant enough."

Douglas grinned from ear to ear, clapped Budd on the back, and chuckled. "Given the circumstances, I suppose they were as pleasant as one could expect. Glad to see you again, old friend!"

Budd saw Evan's eyebrow quirk up toward his hairline at Douglas's comment, for he hadn't mentioned Rose's husband at all in previous weeks. But, alas, the time had finally come where Budd faced the love of his life and his loyalty to Douglas. He hurried and grabbed their luggage from the back of the stagecoach.

"Mr. Thayer set us all up in a house outside of town," Budd explained. "It ain't too far from here. Evan and I will stay in the room just off the kitchen, and you two can have upstairs. Mr. Thayer hopes your time as a ranger will be of good use to our investigation, Douglas."

"I'll do what I can."

Budd walked ahead with Evan, bags tucked under his arms. He said nothing as he led them over to Mr. Thayer's coach, that awaited them all. It would have been easier to hate Douglas, but Budd wished no ill upon his old friend. He simply swallowed his hurt and his pride and forced a smile on his face.

The End

Would you consider leaving a review on Amazon? I would appreciate it.

More westerns are in the works.